x/Western
F
KELL

FINNEY CO. PUBLIC
605 E. WALN
GARDEN CITY, KS

D1162704

FINNEY CO. PUBLIC LIBRARY

184064   Thunder Gods' Gold

APR 11 1994   3/06 (HS)
                          Cl
FEB 13 1996   9/06 (m) EL

NOV - 6 1998
SEP   1 1999

DEMCO

THUNDER GODS' GOLD

AN EVANS NOVEL OF THE WEST

THUNDER GODS' GOLD

LEO P. KELLEY

M. EVANS & COMPANY, INC.   NEW YORK

Library of Congress Cataloging-in-Publication Data

Kelley, Leo P.

  Thunder gods' gold / Leo P. Kelley
  p.   cm.—(An Evans novel of the West)
  ISBN 0-87131-561-0
  I. Title. II. Series.
PS3561.E388T4 1988
813'.54—dc19   88-30149

Copyright © 1988 by Leo P. Kelley

All rights reserved. No part of this book may be reproduced or transmitted
in any form or by any means without the written permission of the publisher.

M. Evans and Company, Inc.
216 East 49 Street
New York, New York 10017

Manufactured in the United States of America

9 8 7 6 5 4 3 2 1

Chapter One

As Dr. Barclay finished binding the dressing on the head of his patient, he said, "That ought to do it, soldier. Come back in a week and we'll have another look to see how it's healing. Meanwhile, you would be well-advised to steer clear of Sergeant Aloysius Molloy."

"Oh, that I will sir. You can count on it. Yes sir, I won't come within a country mile of the bastard—except in the line of duty, of course. If he should make a move to bash in my head for me again, well, I'll just turn tail and run the other way just as fast as my feet can carry me. That's a promise, sir."

"Good day then, Private Simpson."

"It's a good day I bid you, too, sir. Would you care to join me for a drink over to the sutler's, sir?"

"I would but I won't, Simpson. My office hours aren't yet over." Dr. Barclay paused. "You're going to the sutler's for a drink." Another thoughtful pause. "Are you quite sure that's a wise thing to do, Simpson? I mean, isn't that where you had the run-in with Sergeant Molloy yesterday? At the sutler's bar?"

"It is, sir, and I grant you that I may not be making the smartest move of my life going back there, but I have lost a lot of blood from this grievous wound Molloy inflicted on me with his gun butt, so I think it would be wise were I to try to build myself up so I don't get all weak and wishy-washy."

"Whiskey won't build up your blood supply," Barclay said. "But maybe it will give your spirits a boost."

"They badly need just that, sir. Truly it's a boost my spirits are in dire need of, sir. When he put me out like a light with that gun-butt blow of his, Molloy shamed me, he did, in front of all my friends."

"If Molloy should be in the sutler's store when you get there, Simpson—"

"Then I shall leave and forgo a taste of the old red-eye, sir, until another more propitious time. I bid you good day again, sir. My heartfelt thanks to you for the way you've patched up my head. I'm not the brightest man in the world, sir, as you may well have noticed, so I can ill afford to lose any of the little bit of brains the good Lord saw fit to give me."

Barclay smiled as Private Simpson, a bear of a man with a notoriously volatile temper, left the surgery.

The doctor, who was twenty-eight years old, was a tall man who stood exactly six feet in his socks. His slender build tended to disguise the fact that he was a man of great strength, which he sometimes jokingly claimed had developed in medical school when he had had to hold down patients undergoing surgery.

He went to the door of his surgery and looked out into the waiting room. Good, no one there. He could leave a bit early today. Go home and have a talk with Eva. Try to talk some sense into her head and maybe a little warmth into her heart. She'd been so cold of late, so distant. Recently the two of them had moved through the house and their marriage like wary strangers meeting for the first time—always polite, even deferential, but not the least bit friendly. Damn the day it had all begun. That invisible worm of distrust had begun to gnaw in silence and in secret at the hot heart of their love and was destroying it bit by slow but sure bit.

Barclay was about to close the outer door of the waiting room when a soldier came running toward him from the direction of the stables.

"Am I too late, sir?" the man asked breathlessly as he skidded to a halt in front of the doctor. "I'm in need of curing, sir."

"Come in."

When the corporal had followed the doctor into the surgery, Barclay turned and asked, "What can I do for you, soldier?"

The man stood there, nervously twisting his forage cap in his long-fingered hands and refusing to look directly at the doctor.

"Well, son, what is it? I'm no mind reader, and I'm a bad guesser."

"Well sir, Captain Barclay, sir," said the corporal at last, "I reckon I've spent too much time at the hog ranch outside the fort."

"You've got a bad hangover," Barclay said solemnly.

"Oh, no, sir, it's not that at all. A hangover I could manage to cure myself."

"You see, soldier? I told you I was bad guesser."

"Captain," said the corporal, blushing a vivid crimson, "I reckon what I've done is I've gone and got me a bad case of the clap."

"I see." Barclay barely managed to suppress a smile as the corporal fidgeted before him in a fit of embarrassment. "What's your name, by the way?"

"McLane, sir. Orly McLane."

"Well, Orly, let's get to it. If you'll drop your trousers, we'll have a look at you."

Minutes later, after having completed his examination, Barclay said, "We'll begin treatment immediately."

McLane looked shaken. "What're you fixing to do to me, Captain?"

"We'll begin a series of four injections over as many days. Each one will consist of a mixture of potash, bichloride of mercury, and sulfate of quinine."

"Injections?"

Barclay nodded.

"Now I don't want you to think as how I'm a sissy or anything like that, Captain, but I got to ask you, will they hurt?"

"Well, not exactly. But then I feel obligated to warn you that neither are they the most pleasant experiences in the world, since the mixture must be injected directly into the urethra once every twenty-four hours."

"The urethra, Captain?"

Barclay explained.

McLane gave a resigned sigh. "I reckon I danced to the tune, and now it's time to pay the piper."

Barclay smiled. "The wages of sin in this case, Corporal McLane, is not death but something else altogether. Not as deadly but in some ways nearly as unpleasant."

After Corporal McLane left, Barclay dutifully waited fifteen minutes. When no other patients appeared at the door of his surgery, he closed it, made the rounds of the four patients in the attached ten-bed hospital ward, and then left the building which also housed his office, dispensary, kitchen, and storeroom.

He arrived a few minutes later at the small house to which he and his wife, Eva, had been assigned when he had been posted to Fort McDowell in Arizona Territory.

He waved and called out a greeting to his wife, who was seated in a rocker on the veranda, wearing a white linen shirtwaist and a bright blue skirt that hid her feet.

Eva Barclay returned neither her husband's greeting nor his wave. But she did ask, as Barclay joined her in the shade of the veranda, "Are you finished for the day?"

"All finished," he responded, taking a seat on a footstool beside her chair. "I managed to perform one medical miracle today." When his provocative remark brought no response from Eva, he continued, "I was called to the stables. It seems a private on stable duty—quite a strapping fellow—had had a contretemps with a horse, and the soldier, in a fit of pique, punched the horse right between the eyes, knocking the poor beast unconscious.

"The officer in charge of the stables sent for me, thinking the horse had been badly injured. I fretted and fumed over the animal for some time, mumbling medical mumbo jumbo to the officer in charge all the while. When the animal regained consciousness in its own good time, I let everyone think I had brought it back from the dead. A specious medical miracle, I confess to you."

Eva gave her husband a wan smile that in no way matched his ear-to-ear grin.

Barclay took her hand. It was damp with sweat. "What of your day, my darling? Tell me all about it."

"There's really nothing to tell, Ralph. The wind blew, but then it always does out here. It never stops. I dusted this morning. When I was finished, I had to begin again because of that infernal wind that brings a deluge of dust into this house."

"I have an idea, Eva, a perfectly splendid idea! I'll hire a striker."

"I understand that the practice of hiring soldiers as servants has been disallowed by the army."

"Yes, but it is still going on and is being winked at by post commanders everywhere. So I shall do it. I shall hire a striker. I don't want my darling turning into a drudge. It will only cost us between five and ten dollars a month."

"Whatever you think is best, Ralph."

"What I think is best is that you mix more with the other wives on the post. Major Jennings told me only this morning that his wife, Irene, is having a tea party on Wednesday of next week. I'm sure you'll be invited and—"

"I have already been invited."

"You're going, of course."

"Wednesday of next week is days away. I don't like to plan that far ahead."

Barclay tightened his grip on his wife's hand. "You really should get out and socialize more, Eva. Or have people in to tea. You were always quite the social butterfly back in Boston. Remember how you used to stage charades at all those parties you were always giving? Why don't you arrange to have charades performed here at our house some evening? I'm sure everyone would find it most amusing."

Eva slid her hand free of her husband's. She rose and walked to the railing at the far end of the veranda.

From his position on the footstool, Barclay watched her in silence for several minutes as she stood with her arms crossed, her back straight, her shoulders squared. Then, rising, he went to her and placed his hands on her shoulders.

Eva turned to face him.

She was a striking woman—tall and subtly sensuous. At twenty-five her body was firm and decidedly feminine, with full breasts and ample hips. She wore her sleek auburn hair swept up and piled on top of her head, where it was held in place with a tortoiseshell ornament. Her forehead was broad and unlined above penetrating brown eyes. She had fine bones that gave her face a patrician look, as did the smooth, almost translucent skin which covered the elegant bones.

"Ralph, I'm sorry."

He was taken aback. He had not known what to expect from her, but an expression of sorrow—sorrow for what? he wondered—came as a complete surprise.

"Sorry? Whatever for, my darling?"

She met his gaze without wavering, her luminous eyes glowing in the orange light of the setting sun. When she spoke, her voice was strong, the voice of a woman determined to say what was on her mind.

"Ralph, I'm sorry for being such a burden to you."

He was about to speak to her, to protest that she was not a burden, but she held up a hand to silence him.

"I know I've been a complainer and even a scold at times recently. Lord knows, I haven't wanted to be either. I have always despised women who whine. But it seems"—she turned to look off into the distance—"it seems as if I just can't help myself. I keep thinking of all the things Boston is that this place is not. I miss Boston, Ralph, and all that it has to offer. I miss it terribly. I suppose I am not a woman who can deal easily or even readily with hardships of the kind this post, this country, inflicts upon people. You know I grew up in an entirely different world. Perhaps I was pampered.

"Yes, I suppose, now that I think about it, that I was," she continued, speaking softly. "We never wanted for money. We had servants. We had luxuries in that world, Ralph. Here, sometimes the barest necessities of life are not always available. I'm sorry that I haven't borne up well out here. I have tried to. I truly have. But I have come to the reluctant conclusion that I am not a strong woman. I am, sad to say, a weak woman who can do nothing but wither in a world like this, where the sun burns the very blood out of one's body and the wind haunts and hounds one like a—a demon."

"Eva, you're not weak. You've done wonderful things with the house. You've been patient, forbearing, even courageous under what I admit are trying circumstances."

"I made curtains for the windows, yes. Out of muslin, Ralph. Not out of lace or velvet. *Muslin!* It was the only kind of cloth available.

"As for patience, I haven't an ounce of it left to squander on this godforsaken desert. Forbearance? I am no longer forbearing; I am resentful of my—our—lot in life. I was never courageous, Ralph. I have always been afraid of too many things. Of losing your love, for example."

"You will never lose my love, Eva."

"Are you quite sure of that?"

"Why, of course I am."

"Sometimes I wonder. Sometimes I think I have lost it. Or am in the process of losing it."

"I'm afraid I don't at all understand, Eva. Whatever do you mean?"

"You seem to have so little time for me of late, Ralph. If you are not in your surgery or out with the troopers, you have your nose buried in a book. I try to talk to you, and often you don't even hear me. I know you love reading, but I feel shut out sometimes, Ralph."

Barclay took her in his arms and held her close. He whispered into her ear, "It's my fault. I am a hopeless romantic. Give me a good novel and I can lose myself in it for hours—even days—at a time."

"I suppose in some ways each of us has failed the other," Eva said softly, drawing away from Barclay. "I know I have failed you, my dear, and I swear to you that I never ever wanted to do that. Oh, Ralph, I wanted instead to be your safe harbor, your refuge from the wicked of the world who might try to harm you. Instead, I have become—"

"I love you, Eva. I love you more than my life. Do you remember when we were courting? Do you remember how I used to bring you gifts as if gifts could in any conceivable way tell you or show you what was in my heart?"

"I remember that felt doll you bought for my birthday two years ago. Do you remember it? The one that had a defect—those crossed eyes?"

Barclay smiled. "I remember it. I bought it because I thought it looked so forlorn and needed someone loving like you. Do you remember the music box?"

"The one that played that naughty song? Of course I remember it. I was properly shocked by it."

"Go on with you. You *loved* it."

Eva burst into giddy laughter, her hands flying up to cover her mouth. "I confess I did love it. Any other gentleman caller would have brought me something prim and proper, but not you. Oh my, no, not you, my dear. You chose to present me with this perfectly lovely porcelain music box which played—oh, I don't dare repeat those words"

"We had such good times in those days, didn't we?"

"Such very good times."

"We'll have them again once my term of enlistment is up and we return to Boston. By next summer I'll have set up a private practice in a fashionable part of the city and you will have become the toast of the town."

"Won't it be a wonderful day when we leave here?"

"Yes, indeed, it will be. But the days until then can be wonderful, too. We can make them wonderful if we both try hard enough."

Something sparked in Eva's eyes. "I *have* tried to make our times here wonderful, Ralph, but I have failed miserably."

"It's only another year, Eva, and then we will go home."

"Home," she whispered, echoing the word. Tears filled her eyes. She dabbed fiercely at them with her fingers as if they had somehow betrayed her. Then, quickly recovering her composure, she said, "When you finish work tomorrow, Ralph, let's go for a picnic out on the desert. We can watch the sun set. It will be cool then. We'll pretend that we are young lovers who own the whole world and each other. It will be romantic. Shall we, Ralph? Shall we do it tomorrow?"

Barclay silently cursed the turn the conversation had so suddenly taken. "I'm afraid we can't do that, Eva, much as I would like to do it."

"Why not?"

"There are still hostile Indians out there. A great many of them. Only yesterday a scouting party returned with two troopers dead and three wounded. They were attacked by a roving band of Apaches who refuse to live on the land we've provided for them. I'm afraid it would be far too dangerous for us to venture out there alone."

Chapter Two

Eva, a stricken expression on her face, let out a cry that was barely audible. "I feel as if the world is closing in on me. I feel myself to be a prisoner in a world that I have come to loathe."

"Maybe someday soon the army will be able to subdue the hostiles, every man jack of them, and then—"

"*Then*, Ralph? When is *then?* Never mind. It doesn't matter. I am certain that then, whenever then is, will be too late."

When a stolid, expressionless Indian appeared at the edge of the veranda, Barclay was grateful for the interruption. He recognized the man as the leader of one of the tribes of Apaches who, along with some Yavapai Indians, lived on the part of Fort McDowell's military post that had been set aside as a reservation.

"Who is it?" Eva asked uneasily.

"His name is Chunz," Barclay answered. "Excuse me a moment, my dear." Barclay put his hands on the veranda railing and leaned down toward the man. "What can I do for you, Chunz?" he asked.

"You come," the Apache answered and beckoned to Barclay. "Someone in your wickiup is sick, or injured?"

"My woman. You come."

Barclay turned to Eva. "It does appear that my professional duties are not ended for the day, after all. I shall return as soon as possible."

Barclay made his way back to his office, where he collected both his medical and surgical bags since he was not sure what he would be called upon to do. Then he followed Chunz, who strode purposefully between the fort's storehouse and the officers' kitchen. The Apache turned left on the path that passed between the company quarters and the cavalry stables and headed for the domelike wickiups in the distance. Chunz made his way to one that was surrounded by seated women. He entered it with Barclay right behind him.

The Apache pointed at a woman who was lying on a pallet inside the wickiup. "My woman," he said.

"I'll have a look at her." Barclay went to the woman and knelt at her side on the dirt floor.

The woman moaned and slightly raised her left arm.

"She dies," Chunz said dully from behind Barclay.

As if to prove the truth of the Apache's words, the voices of the women outside the wickiup began to wail in what Barclay recognized as a shrill welcome to death, who was, they apparently believed, coming to claim the woman.

He stared down for a moment at the ugly black mass of gangrenous flesh on the woman's left forearm. "What happened?" he asked Chunz as the sickening stench of the woman's rotten flesh caused his stomach to lurch.

"A man came. He try to take her. She would not go. She fought him. He stabbed her."

"Why did you wait so long to come for me?" Barclay asked.

"I bring Apache medicine man here. He stay three days. He do no good. You will do woman good. You will make woman live."

"Chunz," Barclay said, swiveling around to face the man, "I will have to amputate." When he received no response from the puzzled Apache, he explained, "I must cut off the lower part of her injured arm."

"You must do this?"

"Let me put it this way, Chunz. If I do not amputate, she will surely die."

Without hesitation, Chunz said, "Then do what must be done."

Barclay opened his surgical bag. He was aware of Chunz moving closer to him to stare down at the gleaming scalpels, forceps, probing devices, scissors, and bone saw the bag contained. "I will need fire and something of iron to heat in the fire," he told the Apache. "I will need two strong men to hold your woman down while I cut. I will need clean cloths with which to bandage her arm when I am finished."

Chunz turned and left the wickiup. Moments later an Apache woman carrying folded muslin and a long-handled iron spoon entered the wickiup. She handed the cloth and spoon to Barclay and then proceeded to build a fire in the dirt in the center of the wickiup.

When Chunz returned a few minutes later, there was another Apache with him.

After administering morphine to his patient, Barclay placed the handle of the iron spoon in the fire the Apache woman had built and told Chunz and the other man what he wanted them to do.

After both men had knelt down, with Chunz holding on to her legs, the other Apache her arms, Barclay used a scalpel to cut a deep gash all the way around the rotted flesh of his patient's knife wound, baring the bone.

The woman screamed despite the morphine.

Picking up his saw, Barclay began to cut through the bone of the woman's forearm just below the elbow.

Her continuing screams blended with the wild wailing of the mourning women outside the wickiup.

After his saw had bitten through the bone, Barclay set the implement aside. Then, as the woman's left hand and most of her left forearm fell to the ground, she twisted free of the man who was holding her arms. Screaming, her mutilated arm flailing about and spraying blood everywhere, she tried to rise.

The Apache again got a firm grip on her arms and held her still as a blood-spattered Barclay reached behind him and picked up the spoon, the handle of which had turned cherry-red in the fire. He promptly applied it to the bleeding stump of the woman's left arm, searing the arteries and preventing any further loss of blood.

The woman, her eyes rolling wildly in her head so that at times only their whites were visible, arched her back, gave one last piercing scream, and fainted.

Barclay dropped the spoon and picked up the muslin the Apache woman had given him earlier. He ripped it into strips and used it to bandage the crusted stump of the woman's arm. When he had finished, he rose, took a vial from his medical bag, and beckoned to Chunz, who released his hold on the woman's legs and stood up.

Barclay opened the vial and tapped some pills from it into Chunz's hand.

"Give her one of these when she wakes up," he ordered. "Give her another one when the sun rises tomorrow. I will see your woman in the morning. If you should need me before then, send word and I will come."

The hot July sun had surrendered the sky to the moon and stars by the time Barclay returned home.

He entered the main room of the house, where a coal-oil lamp burned, and found that Eva was already in bed in their small bedroom off the kitchen. Outside the windows of the house, the desert wind whistled. What had Eva called the wind—a demon? It sounded like a demon now as it went shrieking past the house on its noisy way to nowhere. The wind, Barclay thought. The desert. Apache Indians. Not much of a life for a man, let alone a woman. Eva was right. He should not have brought her here. He should not have enlisted. He had joined the army out of a sense of duty. It would, he had reasoned, be good for him. It would season him. If he could handle the life of a commissioned officer in the army, he was sure he could handle anything that might befall him and his future patients when he returned to practice in civilized Boston.

He put out the lamp and went into the bedroom. He made more noise than necessary getting undressed, hoping to awaken his wife.

When he climbed into bed next to her, he lay stiff as stone for several minutes, listening to her regular breathing.

Finally he reached out tentatively and touched her shoulder. No response. He gently squeezed her shoulder.

Still no response. But he was sure she was as wide awake now as he was. Had she been awake all along?

More minutes passed.

"Eva?"

"Is something wrong, Ralph?" There was no trace of sleepiness in her voice.

"No, nothing's wrong." Everything is, he thought. "Darling, I know it's late but"—he felt the humiliation that beggars new to their trade must feel—"I want you, Eva." Shame overwhelmed him. He shouldn't have to plead with her. He didn't want to, but desire drove him on. "I *need* you, Eva."

"After you left," she said, "I began to feel ill. I still feel ill. Good night, Ralph."

Barclay's shame gave way to an unreasoning rage. He ground his teeth together so hard his jaws began to ache.

Chapter Three

Dr. Barclay slept fitfully through the night, dozing, awakening, sometimes sleeping deeply while adrift in dark dreams that squeezed sweat from his body and brought fear to his heart.

Long before dawn, he lay wide awake beside his sleeping wife, trying to fight off a feeling of despair over his failing marriage.

Barclay abandoned any hope of sleep. He got out of bed and, carrying his clothes, went into the kitchen, where he lit the lamp and washed before dressing.

From a shelf above the sink he took down his copy of *A Tale of Two Cities* by Charles Dickens. Sitting down at the kitchen table, he drew the lamp closer to him, found his place, and began to read.

Barclay was still reading when the sun rose, unnoticed by him. He was lost in the world of the French Revolution. He heard the cries in the streets of France, heard the tumbrels full of aristocrats rumble through the streets toward the guillotine. He felt the fear of those doomed men and women. He shuddered at the unsettling sight of Madame Defarge and the women with her calmly knitting while blood flooded the gutters of Paris in the holy name of the Revolution.

"Good morning."

The two words were drowned in the loud cries of the eager onlookers as another head fell bloody into the waiting basket beneath the deadly blade of the guillotine and the women's knitting needles clicked and clicked and clicked . . . .

"Ralph!"

Barclay looked up from his book. "Ah, good morning, darling. Did you sleep well?"

"Well enough. Will you have eggs with your bacon this morning?"

Breakfast was a quiet meal in the cramped kitchen. Barclay talked, but he wasn't sure if Eva listened. He told her about the Apache woman he had visited the day before whose arm, through neglect, had become gangrenous.

"I had to amputate," he concluded.

"The poor woman," Eva murmured. "Will she live?"

"I think so. I must go to see her before I report to my surgery. When I think of her and the ills that afflict so many of her people, I count my blessings. When I do, I number you as the foremost among them, Eva."

"Thank you for the pretty compliment, Ralph."

"I didn't mean my remark to be a compliment. I meant—"

Eva looked at him and he fell silent.

What had he meant? He had meant simply that he loved and cherished her. But she had taken it as something a courting cavalier might have whispered into her ear while they were dancing a Virginia reel.

"There was no flour with the provisions that were brought to the fort yesterday," Eva said. "I had hoped to make biscuits." Her words sounded to Barclay like an indictment.

"I must go," he said, blotting his lips with a square of cotton cloth that did duty as a napkin. He rose and was about to kiss Eva on the forehead, but she chose that moment to rise and go to the stove, where she poured herself a cup of coffee.

Barclay left the house and made his way to the Rio Verde, which bordered the fort. It was out of his way, but he wanted to view the river in the light of the rising sun. The flowing water shimmering in the sun had always had a calming affect upon him. By the time he left the river and headed back toward the area of the post given to the Apaches, he was feeling quite peaceful.

Later, as he approached the wickiup Chunz had led him to the day before, he noticed that the mourning women were gone.

He called Chunz's name, and a moment later the Apache appeared in the wickiup's low doorway and beckoned him inside.

"How is she?" Barclay asked Chunz as they both gazed at the woman who was still lying on her pallet, her head turned away from them. Before Chunz could answer the question, the woman turned her head toward them. When she saw who was with Chunz, she smiled.

Barclay also smiled and then knelt beside the woman. With his fingers on her wrist, he felt her pulse. Strong. He took his mon-aural stethoscope and carefully listened to his patient's heartbeat and respiratory functions. Satisfied, he next removed the blood-caked bandages from the woman's arm and examined the stump. He ordered hot water and clean muslin brought, and when they arrived, he cleansed the stump and applied clean bandages.

The woman said something in her language in a voice that was guttural and yet oddly melodious. Barclay glanced at Chunz. The Indian would not meet his gaze.

"Chunz, what did she say?"

When Chunz remained silent, Barclay said, "It might be important. It might be something I should know about her condition."

"It is something you do not need to know."

The woman spoke again, at greater length this time, and it was obvious to Barclay from the woman's agitated state that she was angry with Chunz.

When she fell silent, Chunz, avoiding Barclay's eyes, muttered, "Woman is foolish. Fever troubles her."

"She is not feverish," Barclay stated flatly. "Now, tell me

what she said or I will not continue to care for her."

It was an idle threat, but it worked.

Chunz, after a moment, said, "Woman says you have made the sun shine in her sky again. Now she has light to see Chunz, the man she loves. It was dark for her before you came."

The woman spoke again.

"Chunz?" Barclay prompted.

"Woman says I must give you swift horse or strong Apache woman for what you did for her."

Barclay turned, smiled at the woman, and gently patted her shoulder. As he was about to rise, she took his hand in hers and brought it to her lips. Her ebony eyes met his. Barclay, feeling the soft warmth of her lips on his hand, said, "Chunz, tell her she must get well now so that she may walk again beside the man she loves."

Chunz was still translating Barclay's words as the doctor made his way out of the wickiup. He had already started back toward the hospital when Chunz emerged from the wickiup and called his name.

He waited for Chunz to join him, and when the Apache had done so, he could tell the man had something on his mind.

Finally Chunz said, "She is good woman. For her to die—it would leave a hole in my heart. Maybe I would die too."

"You love her very much."

Chunz nodded. "She tell me to pay you. You heard. You take what you want. I have many horses. See—many women here. Take horse. Take woman."

Barclay, smiling faintly, shook his head. "I thank you, Chunz, for your generous offer. I know the Apaches' ponies are fine mounts. I know, too, of the virtues of the Apache women. But I have a horse, and I already have a wife."

"I must pay you," Chunz insisted. He looked speculatively at Barclay for a moment and then, in a low voice, said, "You will take gold?"

"Gold?"

"*Pesh-la-chi.* Thunder gods' gold."

Barclay's mind began to race. He had heard of the lost bonanzas said to be somewhere in the Superstition Mountains southeast of Fort McDowell. Barclay had heard that the Apaches believed the gold belonged to their thunder gods.

"I pay you with gold," Chunz declared with an air of finality, although Barclay had not spoken. He returned to his wickiup and emerged from it a few minutes later carrying two war bridles made of braided buffalo hair. He beckoned to Barclay, who followed him to a rope corral in which more than a dozen horses milled or stood idly about.

Chunz ducked down under the rope and entered the corral, where he quickly looped the bridles around the lower jaws of the two horses he had selected. He led them from the corral and handed the bridle of one of the animals to Barclay.

The bemused doctor looked at the bare back of the horse whose bridle he was holding and then at Chunz. "Am I expected to ride this horse without a saddle?"

"You ride. Like Indian you ride." Chunz leaped onto the back of his mount and sat there watching Barclay. He was obviously waiting for the doctor to board his horse.

Barclay, who had never ridden a horse bareback in his life, hesitated. But his hesitation abruptly vanished when he thought of the gold to which Chunz had promised to take him.

He tried leaping onto his horse as he had seen Chunz do. On his first attempt, he failed to seat himself and slid back off the mount he had almost spooked. His second attempt also ended in failure. But on his third try, he managed to land on the horse's back, where he remained.

Chunz moved out, traveling southeast along the western bank of the Rio Verde.

Barclay, experimenting with the unfamiliar bridle, gradually was able to gain control of his mount. He urged it into a canter and caught up with Chunz.

With his knees gripping the barrel of his mount to keep himself from falling, he couldn't help wondering if he had embarked on a wild-goose chase.

Barclay felt sweat break out on his face and body although the day was not yet hot. Immediately afterward, he felt a chill. Racing through his mind were all the stories he had heard about lost mines and diggings that were said to be hidden in the Superstitions.

To steady himself, he glanced at Chunz riding next to him and asked, "What's this about thunder gods?"

"Thunder gods live in mountains," Chunz replied matter-of-factly. "We Apache guard their gold for them. Keep it from men who would steal it—white men."

Barclay heard the unmistakable contempt with which the Indian had uttered the last two words. "Then why are you taking me to the gold?" he inquired uneasily. "Won't what you're doing make your thunder gods angry?"

Chunz shook his head. "I speak to thunder gods when we get there. I tell them what I do and why I do it. They will not harm us."

"Have no other white men ever found the gold you are taking me to?"

"White men find. Apache find white men."

Chunz's words chilled Barclay. He thought of what the Indians had done to the two men who were on patrol the day before yesterday. A stark image of the men's mutilated bodies flared in his mind and sickened his stomach.

He thought of turning back now before it was too late. But the gold . . . He rode on

Around him the desert lay seemingly lifeless under the sun. But the land was actually very much alive. The half-mile-long stretch of saguaro cactus proved that. So did the single towering soap tree yucca in the distance and the prairielike grasses that in some places were nearly as high as the ankles of a man on horseback. Animal life—pack rats and other rodents—would come out when the sun went down and the desert turned cold. Then the desert would be truly alive, Barclay knew from his times on night patrol with the troopers. Now the only sign of life, other than plant life, was a collared lizard running from an unseen enemy on its long hind legs, its body upright, its head thrust forward.

It was Chunz who first saw the small band of Apaches. He pointed them out to Barclay.

"I see nothing," Barclay said, shielding his eyes and staring in the direction the Apache had indicated. "What is there, Chunz?"

"Apaches. You look close."

Barclay did. Still he saw nothing.

"Apaches on ground near ocotillo bushes."

Barclay was finally able to make out the forms of the four Indians as they lay on the ground, seeming to blend in with it.

"They're watching us," he told Chunz, apprehension causing his voice to quaver. "Will they attack us?"

"Man in front—Eskiminzin. He and men with him, they not come to fort. Live wild. You stay here."

Barclay halted his horse and remained where he was as Chunz rode toward the renegade Apaches.

He continued watching as Chunz drew rein and Eskiminzin and the other three Apaches rose to their feet and gathered around him.

Chunz turned and pointed to the southeast. Then he pointed to Barclay, who, seeing the gesture, froze, his hands rigid on his reins.

He relaxed only when the four Apaches who had been speaking with Chunz moved away and disappeared into the landscape.

"They will not harm us, will they?" Barclay asked apprehensively when he and Chunz resumed their journey.

"No. I tell Eskiminzin I take you to gold. I tell why I do this. Eskiminzin and his men will not harm us. But you must never come here again to look for gold. If you do and Eskiminzin or his braves see you, they will kill you. They have killed other white men who would take away thunder gods' gold."

As the journey continued, the sun rose higher in the cloudless sky. To Barclay, its heat was a hammer pounding his skull. Why had he not thought to bring a canteen full of water? Why had not Chunz suggested that he do so? He glanced at the Apache, who had an impassive, almost serene expression on his face. Barclay wondered why the man did not sweat.

By the time they reached the juncture of the Rio Verde and the Salt river seven miles south of Fort McDowell, Barclay's throat was so dry he could barely swallow.

He refused to think about it. He thought instead about the gold. He was still thinking about the gold when they crossed the Salt River near Mormon Flat ford and began riding past the mouths of some canyons which led down from the Superstition Mountains.

Barclay was beginning to believe he was indeed about to become a rich man, and he found himself thinking of the future. In a year, once he was discharged from the army, he would return with Eva to Boston, there to establish himself as a physician in private practice. They would begin to raise a family, if no child had been born to him and Eva before that time.

The gold would insure them more than just wealth. It would, despite what the old saw said, buy him and Eva happiness. He was convinced of it.

When she saw the golden treasure, Eva's eyes would light up with joy. She would do a little dance of joy, twirling about, her arms flung out, her head thrown back. The gold would make up for all the hardships she had suffered. It would be her deliverance.

Chunz suddenly brought his horse to a halt, and Barclay did the same.

Chunz moved his horse closer to Barclay's and untied a blue bandanna that he wore around his neck. "You may not know the way to gold," Chunz declared solemnly. "You must wear this so that you cannot tell where gold is."

Barclay laughed nervously. "Wouldn't it have been much simpler if you had just gotten some of your thunder gods' gold and given it to me yourself? I mean, instead of all this rigmarole?"

"Apache dare not take gold. It belong to thunder gods. To take gold—that would be very bad for Apache. Thunder gods would punish Apache for stealing gold."

Before Chunz could tie the blindfold around Barclay's head,

the doctor quickly scanned the topography of the area—the four peaks off to the west, the growth of scrub pine and ocotillo at the canyon's entrance, the creek that formed a tiny waterfall not far away.

Then the blindfold was securely in place and he could see nothing more. But as they moved out again, he concentrated his attention on the twists and turns the trail took—now to the right, now sharply left—and he paid close attention to the sound of his pony's hooves, which now struck granite, then sank in sand. He listened to the laborious breathing of his mount as the animal climbed higher into cooler air. He heard the clatter of its hooves as it crossed an expanse of rock-strewn ground. For a while the sun was on his face; later, for a longer time, it was on his back. He remained conscious of the time passing so that when Chunz halted his mount and removed Barclay's blindfold, he estimated that they had been climbing for nearly two hours.

The doctor blinked in the blaze of the sun until he grew accustomed to the bright light. Then, looking around, he saw that they had stopped in a narrow north–south-running canyon, the western wall of which was formed by the soaring cliffs of a long mountain.

Chunz dismounted and indicated that Barclay was to do the same. Then, raising both arms and tilting his face upward, Chunz began to intone in the Apache language what Barclay assumed was a prayer to his deities. Perhaps it was a plea asking that they be allowed to pass safely to the spot where the thunder gods' gold lay hidden.

Then, with Chunz in the lead, the two men headed up a steep tributary canyon which seemed at first to Barclay to end at the sheer wall of the overhanging cliffs. But as he neared the cliffs, Barclay saw that the smaller canyon led down to a small valley that had hitherto been hidden from sight.

Chunz moved lithely down the incline.

Barclay, arms akimbo as he struggled to maintain his footing on the unstable ground, followed him down into the shallow valley.

FINNEY CO. PUBLIC LIBRARY
605 E. WALNUT
GARDEN CITY, KS 67846

When Barclay reached his side, Chunz pointed mutely, and Barclay looked to see shards of sunlight gleaming in the distance. He knew instantly what the light meant. Gold! The sunlight was reflecting off the bright yellow metal that was embedded in a long ledge of rose-colored quartz.

When the doctor reached the spot, he dropped to his knees like a worshipper in a rocky church and stared in wonder at the bonanza that lay before him. Then, moving as if in a dream, he reached down and picked up a piece of quartz that had fallen from the ledge. He ran an index finger along the gold in the formation.

Then, letting out a yell, he leaped to his feet. Holding the quartz up to the sun so that it glinted and glittered in the bright light, he let out another wild yell, a kind of victory cry.

He turned back to the vein of gold and, using the piece of quartz in his hand as a makeshift hammer, he began to pound on the surface of the ledge. He succeeded in chipping away small pieces of quartz, but the work was hard and the yield unsatisfying.

Why hadn't he come prepared with a pick or a knife, at least? A knife.

He remembered having noticed . . .

He turned to Chunz, his eyes on the sheathed knife the Indian wore on his belt. He looked up at Chunz. Before he could ask to borrow the knife, Chunz wordlessly unsheathed the weapon and handed it to him.

Barclay gratefully took it and knelt. He used the knife, at first somewhat clumsily, but then, as he gained experience, with a fair degree of skill as he set about prying the malleable gold from the quartz that held it prisoner.

He gradually became aware of the soft roar of thunder in the distance, but the threat of rain did not deter him in the least.

He had no idea how long he had worked or how much time had passed until his coat and trouser pockets were completely full and unable to hold another flake of gold. He looked up at the sky. The sun was at the meridian.

The sun?

But he had heard thunder, hadn't he?

And yet there wasn't a cloud in the sky and the only sound Barclay now heard was a flicker steadily pecking at a nearby tree.

He tried desperately to stuff another nugget into one of his pockets. It wouldn't fit. He tore off his coat, tied the ends of its sleeves together, and began to fill the arms with more gold.

He picked up another piece of quartz, intending to pound it with a rock he had found. He decided it was too small. He abandoned it in favor of a large piece of quartz which contained far more gold.

An hour later he groaned when the sleeves of his coat were stuffed full of gold ore. No more room, he thought sadly. *Next time I'll bring saddlebags, tarpaulins—anything I can find to carry the gold home in.*

Next time . . . The two words roared in his mind. He glanced surreptitiously at Chunz, who was watching him, an unreadable expression on his dark face.

Barclay rose, his riches weighing him down, and walked stiffly and slowly to his horse, the sleeves of his coat and all of his pockets full of gold ore that was going to make all his—and Eva's—dreams come true.

He had a great deal of trouble mounting his horse, but he finally managed to do so. When Chunz had blindfolded him again, the two men rode back the way they had come, Barclay trying to force himself to pay attention to the terrain, to how the sun struck his body and face, to the occasional lack of sunlight which meant a rock formation had temporarily blotted out the sun, but he could not concentrate. Not on his surroundings, at any rate. He could, however, concentrate on the gold he was carrying.

He remembered the stories he had heard when he was a boy about the men who went west to the California goldfields to try to find their fortunes. There had been exciting tales of men who struck it rich, and sad tales of men who never had any luck worth mentioning. He was happy now, nearly thirty years later, to have found a golden treasure that was just as rich as those of the fabled days of 1849.

Chapter Four

After returning to Fort McDowell, Barclay returned Chunz's horse and made his way directly to his office, where he removed the ore from his pockets and the sleeves of his coat. Then he left the office and went to the stables, where he borrowed a hammer from the smithy on duty and a burlap bag from the private who was cleaning out the stalls.

Once back in his office, he waited for darkness to descend and then carried some of the ore, together with a lighted lamp, outside and around to the rear of the building.

For the next several hours he diligently pounded the fragments of rose quartz with the hammer in order to retrieve the gold inside. By the time he had finished the task to his satisfaction, the ground at the rear of the medical building was strewn with small pieces of quartz, and the burlap bag Barclay had obtained was half full of coarse gold in various shapes, ranging in size from wheat kernels to melon seeds.

Barclay carried the bag into his office, where he placed it on his desk. Only then did he allow himself to relax and realize that he was exhausted.

Exhausted but also exhilarated. He felt more alive, despite his fatigue, than he could ever remember feeling in his life. He knew he should go home and get some sleep, but he was just as sure he wouldn't be able to sleep. And, if he did go home, he would have to talk to Eva, and he didn't want to do that. Not yet. He didn't want to tell her of the fabulous good fortune that had befallen them. Tomorrow would be time enough to spring his happy surprise on her. After he had taken the next step in the plan he had been formulating in his mind during the return trip from the Superstition Mountains.

He supposed Eva would be worried about him. She would wonder why he had not returned home as usual when his office hours ended. Well, he thought with a self-satisfied smile, her worries would soon be over, all of them.

He rose and made himself as comfortable as possible on the couch in his waiting room. He had no sooner done so than he fell into a deep, contented sleep.

Barclay awoke from a surprisingly pleasant dream of drowning in a golden waterfall the next morning and shouted to whoever it was who was pounding on his office door, "I'm coming, dammit! I'm coming!"

He got up from the couch, straightened his clothes as best he could, brushed back his hair, and opened the outer door to find a private standing on the doorstep.

"Sir, I'm feeling real poorly," said the private, who was pale and sweaty.

Ten minutes later, Barclay's diagnosis was that the soldier was suffering from pneumonia. He admitted the man to the hospital.

His day had begun.

Throughout it, he had to force himself to concentrate on what he was doing because his thoughts kept returning to the bag of gold he had placed on his desk. Between patient visits, he imagined himself and Eva traveling to Cairo to see the Pyramids and the Sphinx, imagined them sipping cold ices under a fat Venetian sun, imagined them returning from their grand tour to a place of their own where they reigned supreme.

Finally his day in the office came to an end.

When it did, he picked up the burlap bag containing the gold and carried it across the parade ground to the office of the quartermaster.

Once there, he placed the bag on the counter and addressed the quartermaster. "Sergeant Levine, I take it the government is still buying gold?"

"Oh, yes, sir. Indeed they are, sir. They are greedy for gold, and I imagine they will be till the last trump. Have you some to sell, sir?"

With a flourish, Barclay indicated the burlap bag resting on the counter.

The sergeant opened it and peered inside.

Barclay, amused, watched the man's eyes widen and his lips part to form an astonished O.

The sergeant looked up at Barclay and said, "Sir, this is for sure and certain an embarrassment of riches, as they say. Wherever in the world did you come upon such a bonanza as this?"

"I was doing some prospecting, Sergeant, and I had a bit of luck."

The sergeant did not pursue the matter. Instead he got out his scale and proceeded to weigh the gold.

The process was time-consuming both because of the quantity of gold to be weighed and also because of the sergeant's slow and meticulous manner of writing down in a green ledger the exact weight of each batch of gold and what it was worth in dollars.

When the task was finally finished, the sergeant, wetting the lead point of his pencil with his tongue, tallied the column of figures he had written in his ledger. Then he looked up at Barclay and said, "It comes to eleven thousand dollars for the whole shebang, sir."

Barclay, wanting to shout his delight, restrained himself with a mighty effort and merely said, "A tidy sum."

"Indeed it is, sir," enthused the sergeant as he proceeded to unlock a cash box, counted out the sum due, and handed it over.

Barclay stuffed the thick wad of paper money into his pocket, bade the sergeant good evening, and left.

His next stop was at the office of the commanding officer of Fort McDowell.

He told the corporal who was seated outside the office of the commanding officer that he had urgent business with Colonel Carstair.

The corporal went into the inner office and returned a moment later to usher Barclay into the presence of Colonel Henry Carstair.

"Captain Barclay, it's good to see you" said the beefy commanding officer of the post, rising from the chair behind his desk and offering his hand.

As the two men shook hands, Carstair asked, "What's the trouble?"

"No trouble, sir. I just came to arrange for a furlough."

Carstair sat down again and waved Barclay into a chair on the opposite side of his desk. "How much leave time do you require, Captain?"

Barclay had been about to ask for a week, but he said instead, "Two weeks, sir."

"Two weeks," Carstair repeated, thoughtfully stroking his bearded chin. "When do you want your furlough to begin?"

"Tomorrow, sir, if that's possible."

"Rather short notice, Captain," Carstair commented. "But we can manage. We'll have to find someone to replace you while you're gone. If it were a day or two—even a week—we could probably send the men on sick call to Camp Verde, but two weeks is a long time for such an operation. No, I'd best telegraph to Camp Verde and have them assign one of their medical officers to us while you're gone."

"I'm sorry to put you to so much trouble."

"No trouble at all, really. We'll manage without you. That

should teach you a lesson in humility, Captain. No man is indispensable. I sometimes find myself believing that I am. That this fort could not function without me. But I know down deep in my heart such is not at all the case. Why, this post would be running smoothly and efficiently should I die, I wager—"

"Sir, I'm sorry to interrupt but I really must be going. My wife is waiting for me."

"Of course. I understand. Give my very best regards to your lovely helpmate, Captain."

The two men shook hands again and Barclay left the office.

Once outside, he ran all the way home.

When he got there, he found Eva scrubbing the plank floor of the kitchen on her hands and knees.

She looked up at him as he burst through the door and then down again at the soapy floor.

"Eva, I have news—wonderful news!"

She rubbed the bar of yellow soap against the stiff bristles of the scrub brush she was holding and continued cleaning the floor, wisps of her hair falling down around her face.

"Have you?" she said. "I'm rather surprised that you found the time to come home to tell your good news to me."

"You're upset. I suppose you have a right to be. I should have sent word that I wouldn't be home last night. But you see I didn't want to do that because—"

"Where did you spend the night? At that house of ill repute near the post?"

Barclay was taken aback by her question. For a moment he was unable to answer it. He was shocked that she thought he had gone to that place, to a prostitute.

"I understand," Eva said evenly. "After all, I haven't been the most devoted wife lately. I can hardly blame you for—"

"Eva, I spent last night in my office."

She gave him a searching look. "Why, Ralph?"

He began to smile. He bent down and took the soap and scrub brush from her hands, dropping them both in the bucket of water. He took her arms and helped her to her feet.

When she stood facing him, he said, "We are rich, my darling."

She frowned. "Rich?"

He thrust a hand into his pocket, pulled out the money he had received from the quartermaster in exchange for the gold, and held it out to her.

She took it from him, looked down at it, and then up at him again. "Where did you get all this money, Ralph?"

"You really needn't look at me like that, Eva. I didn't go to Phoenix and rob a bank to get it. I found it. Well, not the money itself. I mean I found the means to get the money."

"Ralph, I don't know what you're talking about."

Despite his excitement, Barclay forced himself to speak slowly. "You remember Chunz, who came here the day before yesterday?" When Eva nodded, Barclay continued, "You remember that I had to amputate a portion of his wife's arm."

Eva nodded again. "But what has that to do with this?" She held up the money in her hand.

"Be patient. I shall explain. I think it best to begin at the beginning. Now then"—Barclay drew a deep breath—"Chunz was so grateful to me for having saved his woman's life that he wanted to give me a reward of some sort."

"*He* gave you this money? But how could he? I mean, there must be thousands of dollars here."

"Eleven thousand, to be exact. Chunz didn't give it to me. Well, in a sense I suppose you could say he did. Let me explain. When I told him I didn't want the horse or the Apache wife he offered me, he volunteered to take me to a site in the Superstition Mountains where he said there was a great deal of gold. Well, take me he did. And he was right. There was a fabulously rich vein of gold running through a long ledge of rose quartz."

When he finally finished his account of how he had obtained the money, Eva laughed, threw her arms around him, and hugged him. He hugged her back, both of them laughing happily now. They twirled in a circle, still locked in an embrace.

Eva suddenly lost her balance. She seized Barclay's shoulder to steady herself, and as she did the money fell from her hand and fluttered to the floor.

"Oh!" she cried in giddy dismay. As she bent to pick it up, she slipped on the soapy floor and fell.

"Are you hurt?" Barclay asked, immediately solicitous as he dropped to his knees beside her.

"No," she answered, sitting up and smiling happily at her husband. "Oh, Ralph, it's true. We're rich."

"And we shall be richer." As he picked up the money, Barclay enthusiastically described in detail to Eva what he had seen before and what he had sensed after having been blindfolded by Chunz during their journey into the mountains. He briefly mentioned their encounter with the renegade Apaches led by Eskiminzin and described Chunz's tale of the Indians' thunder gods.

When he fell silent, Eva stared at him, a concerned expression on her face. After a tense moment, she began, "You mean—"

"I told you, Eva. There is an almost limitless amount of gold there in the mountains. I was able to carry only a small portion of ore back to the post. But next time—"

"Next time, Ralph?"

"Next time I'll be better prepared. I'll go to Phoenix first and buy a pack mule and tools to build an *arrastra* to crush the ore right there on the spot. That way I can bring back great quantities of gold packed on the mule instead of chunks of raw ore that require crushing here. King Croesus will seem like a piker compared to us, Eva, when I—"

"Then you are going back into those mountains."

"Why, yes. Of course I am." Barclay stared at his wife in surprise. Had she ever doubted that he would go back? Didn't she understand that he *had* to go back? "I've already arranged with Colonel Carstair for a two-week leave."

"You told me you saw Apaches on your way to the mountains. A band of them led by a man named—what did you say his name was?"

"Eskiminzin."

"If Chunz had not been with you to give you safe conduct, so to speak, this Eskiminzin and his men might have killed you. You told me Chunz said those Apaches would kill you if they discovered you had returned to the area to search for the gold you found there."

"Yes, but—"

"Yet now you talk about leaving the fort and going back to the mountains alone, when only the day before yesterday you told me we didn't dare go outside the fort for a picnic because of the presence of hostile Indians in the area."

"Eva, this is no picnic that I'm going on. This is something important. It is something very important to both of us and to our future together. It is something I must do."

"At the risk of losing your life?"

"I shall take a weapon with me this time. I shall be careful."

"What about the curse?"

"Curse? What curse? What are you talking about?"

"You told me Chunz said the gold is protected by the Apaches for their thunder gods, that the thunder gods would curse anyone who dared to take it from them without permission."

"Perhaps I didn't make myself clear. Chunz did not mention a curse. He did say that the gold belongs to his thunder gods—"

"He blindfolded you on the way there and on the way back so that you would not be able to find the spot where the gold is located. You said he told you that he didn't want you to know where the location is. Don't you think he or the other Apaches will take action against you if they should find out that you have gone back to steal—"

"Eva, stop it! I am not stealing anybody's gold. Certainly not any thunder gods' gold. One cannot steal from mythical beings who do not exist except in the naive minds of primitive savages. The gold is a mineral. It lies there in the mountains waiting for any man who can claim it. And I intend to claim all of it, if I can manage to do so."

"You say you will take a weapon with you when you return. But, Ralph, you are not an expert with a gun. Then, too, you are only one man against a group of renegade Apaches who, if they discover what you are planning to do, wouldn't hesitate to kill you."

"I've told you, Eva. I shall be armed and I shall be careful."

"Ralph, you are no mountain man who knows how to survive out there in the wilderness. You are not an Indian fighter. You're a doctor, a healer."

His wife's words stirred anger deep within Barclay.

"Stay here, Ralph. Don't be foolish."

Barclay's anger grew, but his face remained impassive.

"Eva," he said, "this is a once-in-a-lifetime opportunity. I can't afford to ignore or miss it." He began to pick up the money, some of which was damp as a result of having fallen on wet parts of the floor.

"This eleven thousand dollars that we have safely in hand— Ralph, be content with it. When we get back to Boston, you'll be able to earn a great deal of money over time in private practice. We don't need any more money. Not if it means risking your life to get it. Don't you see?"

Barclay's face flushed as his anger suddenly erupted into rage. He stuffed the money he had retrieved back into his pocket and stood up without offering to help Eva to her feet.

"You don't think I'm capable of getting the gold out of the mountains, do you?"

"I didn't say that. I said—"

"You said I was no mountain man. You don't think I'm much of a man of any kind, do you, Eva? Certainly not enough of a man to brave a few hostiles and come away with a bonanza that few men would dare even to dream about, never mind manage to possess. No, don't say anything more. I'm going and that's all there is to be said on the matter. Maybe you're right. Maybe I'm not a Jim Bridger—but I am a *man,* Eva, and perfectly capable of doing a man's job."

"You haven't understood me. I did not say you are at all unmanly. I merely said that—"

But Barclay stormed out of the house before hearing any more of what Eva had to say to him.

Standing outside the house in the gathering gloom, he wasn't sure what to do next. He could return to his office and spend another night there, but the prospect was not at all appealing. He began to walk, aimlessly at first, but then, after a few minutes, with purpose.

He arrived at the sutler's store to find it aglow with lamplight and cheerful with the sounds of song accompanied by a lone man playing an out-of-tune fiddle. Two men danced a rowdy hornpipe in the middle of the rectangular room. Their shadow leaped on the walls.

Barclay made his way through the smoky haze to the bar at one end of the room. He ordered bourbon, and when the sutler had placed a nearly full glass in front of him, he tossed it down and ordered a refill, which was promptly provided. This one he sipped.

Barclay raged inwardly that Eva had no right talking to him the way she had. She had talked as if he were incapable of taking care of himself in the wilderness. Granted he was not used to doing so. But a man could learn, couldn't he? A man could do anything he had to do if he just set his mind to doing it and doing it well. Which is exactly what he intended to do, and no nagging wife or renegade Apaches were going to stop him. He downed his second drink.

Barclay indicated impatiently to the sutler that he wanted another drink. It was poured. He silently toasted his good fortune, and then his future good fortune—the success of his planned venture.

As the bourbon boiled within him, he turned from the bar to survey the crowd again. A post laundress was leading a man up the steps to the second floor.

The sight of the pair caused a pang of loneliness in Barclay. The laundress was not unattractive. The sight of her made him think of the brothel outside the fort. He had never been there, but Eva had accused him of having spent the previous night there. *Might as well be damned as much for what I do as for what I didn't,* he told himself.

He paid for his drinks and was about to leave the sutler's store when the door opened and in walked Sergeant Levine, the quartermaster. To Barclay, who knew none of the other people in the room, Levine seemed like an old friend. He hailed the man and the quartermaster quickly joined him at the bar.

"What'll you have to drink, Sergeant Levine?" Barclay asked, beckoning to the sutler, who was serving a customer at the far end of the bar.

"Whiskey'll do me just fine, Captain."

When the sutler placed the drink before Levine, the sergeant raised his glass and offered a toast. "To your great good fortune, Captain."

Barclay smiled, the bourbon he had drunk a cheerful tide buoying him. "I'll have another bourbon," he told the sutler. When the idea occurred to him, he wondered why he hadn't thought of it before. "And see to it that everyone has a drink on me," he ordered. "A man as fortunate as I am should spread his largess among others not quite so fortunate, don't you think?"

The sutler did indeed think so and said so enthusiastically, since Barclay's idea definitely was good for business.

Soon a crowd had gathered around Barclay and Sergeant Levine. It was the sergeant who expansively answered the questions put to Barclay. The doctor was pleased to let the man deal with the task, preferring to bask in the sunny warmth that had been born of the bourbon he had consumed.

"Gents, the captain is a rich man, thanks to the gold he found and sold to me today—to the United States government, to put it precisely—for eleven thousand dollars."

As if to prove Levine's statement, Barclay withdrew the money from his pocket and held it up for the crowd to see.

They cheered, and then the magic word "gold" began to pass from one pair of lips to the next. It was followed by other words such as "When did he find it?" and "Where did he find it?" By such words as "How much did he find?" and "The lucky son of a bitch."

Barclay noticed the envy in the eyes of a young bugler standing nearby, and it pleased him. He noticed too the appraising stare of a sergeant not far away who had shoulders as wide as a barn door and hands like hams. He noticed the laundress, back from her labors, push her way through the crowd. She linked her arm in his and asked, "What's all the excitement about, honey?" Sergeant Levine told her.

She *ooohhed*, and Barclay, aware that he was quite drunk now but not caring, pulled a ten-dollar bill from his pocket and playfully tucked it into the bodice of the laundress's dress, which revealed a tantalizing amount of cleavage. She kissed him on the cheek. A few minutes later, when Barclay felt her small hand try to slide surreptitiously into his pocket, he promptly pulled it out and chided her with a wagging finger and a melodramatic frown. She pouted prettily and then flounced away from him in search of other prey.

He bought another round of drinks for the house. He was slapped on the back. He was hailed as a fellow well-met. He felt loved and wanted and needed. And drunk.

He had another drink. What the hell and why not?

The young bugler appeared beside him, wrapped an arm around his shoulder, and asked where the gold was to be found. He liked the young bugler. He wanted him to know where the gold was. He wasn't selfish; there was enough for everybody. He wanted to tell him, but the words wouldn't come. His tongue had become leaden in his mouth. He made a gurgling sound. The young bugler swore and vanished.

Some time later, so did Sergeant Levine.

Barclay weaved his way toward the door, which appeared to him to be two, then three doors. Putting out his hands to grab one of the three wooden latches that danced in the air before his drunken eyes, he missed them all. He staggered and nearly fell.

"Steady, Captain," said the sutler, a wavy apparition appearing suddenly at his side. "Let me unlatch the door for you."

Barclay went out into the night. The chilly air was a sweet relief after the choking smoke of the sutler's store. He breathed deeply, steadied himself, and started for his office.

Where was everyone? Gone, all of them gone into the night, he supposed, deserters all. Sergeant Levine. The young bugler. The laundress. The sergeant with the big hands and big shoulders who had been watching him. Or was *he* the deserter? Were they all still there in the golden lamplight of the store.

He turned back, his eyes on the lighted windows of the store. The door of the store opened. He halted and saw the young bugler come out. Beside him was another man Barclay vaguely recalled having seen talking to the bugler earlier. He raised a hand, tried to beckon. He belched.

When he looked again, the two men had disappeared. They had vanished, he realized a moment later with some chagrin, because he had inadvertently stumbled into the passageway that ran between the company quarters and the officers' quarters.

He was disoriented. He wanted only to lie down somewhere and sleep until the alcoholic fumes were driven from his benumbed brain.

He shouldn't have drunk so much so quickly. He seldom drank alcoholic beverages. The last time had been more than six months ago at Christmastime.

He smiled, remembering the decorations on the Christmas tree—a young palo verde tree and not the traditional evergreen. He had helped Eva make the strings of popcorn and cranberries, the looped and pasted chains of colored paper for their tree.

"There he is!"

Barclay turned toward the spot he thought the whispered words had come from. Who was out there, hidden in the dark?

His stomach constricted. His skin crawled. He saw no one, heard not another sound. He turned and tried to run but managed little more than a shuffling walk.

Someone was running after him. He could hear him. No, them—two pairs of running feet. Looking back over his shoulder he saw the two indistinct figures running after him. He moved as fast as he could.

But not fast enough.

As both caught up with him, one of the men seized his shoulder and jerked him backward so hard and so swiftly that he almost fell.

"What—" he cried, his own voice unfamiliar to his ears, so hoarse with fright and cracked with fear was it.

"The money," one of the men muttered. "The eleven thousand dollars Sergeant Levine said he paid you," said the other man. The sudden appearance of the nearly full moon behind a cloud bank revealed him to be the young bugler.

"Hand it over," said the other man, whom Barclay had seen the bugler speaking to in the store.

"No," Barclay said. "I won't give it to you."

"Yes," said the young bugler and struck him in the mouth with his right fist. "You will give it to us." ·

As Barclay staggered backward, his lip broken and bleeding, he thrust a protective hand into his pocket, determined not to surrender the money he had gotten in exchange for the gold.

Chapter Five

"Look," said the exasperated bugler, "just give us the money and you won't get hurt."

"No," Barclay repeated, his fingers encircling the money in his pocket as he backed away.

The bugler's companion darted forward and around behind the doctor. A moment later Barclay felt the man's forearm become a strong, sinewy bar across his throat.

Gagging as his attacker proceeded to choke him, Barclay fought desperately to tear the man's arm away from his throat. He clawed with both hands at the obstruction that was cutting off his air, but it remained firmly in place.

The bugler, who still maintained an aggressive stance in front of him, suddenly drew back his right fist and rammed it into Barclay's stomach.

The doctor, gasping for breath, felt the darkness around him deepen, and he realized that he was about to lose consciousness. Desperate, he stopped trying to free himself from the forearm that was pressing against his throat and slammed an elbow into the gut of the man behind him.

The maneuver worked. The man released his hold on Barclay and doubled over in pain.

The bugler again struck Barclay in the stomach. This time the blow so sickened Barclay that he vomited.

The bugler cursed as he was befouled by the doctor.

The man behind Barclay seized him by the throat and, swearing volubly, threatened to break his neck. Suddenly sober, Barclay reached behind him, seized the man's wrists, and bent sharply forward. Then, with an abrupt jerk that required all the strength he possessed, he threw his attacker over his head. When the man hit the ground in front of him, Barclay made a run for it, his legs pumping like pistons.

He considered calling for help. He was sure that if he survived this encounter, Eva would say that was what he should do. The thought of her saying so made him determined he would not call for help. If he could not keep his money through his own efforts, he decided he didn't deserve to keep it.

Barclay didn't get far before both men were on him again, and this time, with an icy sense of panic, Barclay saw the moonlight glint on the sharp blade of a Bowie knife in the right hand of the bugler. Before he could make a move, the blade flew toward him and he cried out in pain as it sliced into his left biceps.

"We want the money!" the bugler barked. "You got yourself a choice, Doc. You can hand it over and live, or you can keep it and die."

"Nobody's dying here tonight, unless it's one of you two bad boys," came a resonant voice from the darkness.

Before Barclay could see who it was, the bugler was knocked headlong to the ground. The knife flew from his hand, and a third man, who was taller than either of Barclay's attackers, turned on the man who had tried to choke the doctor. A smashing right uppercut and a hard left cross knocked that man to the ground. The bugler got to his feet and tried to defend himself, but the tall man clenched his hands together and brought them down on top of the bugler's head. His knees buckled and he went down, but he got up again quickly and helped his companion to his feet. Then both men fled into the night.

"Let's get out of here, sir," said the man who had come to Barclay's aid.

"The hospital," Barclay said.

They made their way there. Once inside, Barclay set about treating his own knife wound. He said, "They tried to rob me. The bugler said he was going to kill me if I didn't hand over my money to them."

"Ah, so the bastards took it from you, did they?"

Barclay wearily shook his head. "No, they didn't get it."

"Isn't that good news now?"

"It's thanks to you that they didn't get it."

"I'm just glad I came upon the scene when I did, Captain Barclay."

"You have me at a disadvantage. I don't know your name, although I recall seeing you in the sutler's store earlier this evening." Barclay realized he was talking to the sergeant he had seen watching him so intently.

"My name is Sergeant Benjamin Pardue, Captain. It's pleased I am to make your acquaintance."

Sergeant Pardue was broad-shouldered and barrel-chested. He towered several inches over Barclay. His full beard was brown, but the lamplight revealed reddish highlights in it. He had a hearty way of speaking, and when he talked, his eyes seemed to shine. He looked to Barclay as if he were about to burst out of the clothes he was wearing.

"The bugler and that other man," Barclay remarked, "must have followed me when I left the sutler's."

"They did that, sir. When I saw them leave, I said to myself, Pardue, the captain—you'll pardon me, sir, for saying this—he's had himself a snootful of the oh-be-joyful and it has loosened his tongue such that those two suspicious-looking wolves are on the prowl for the poke he's been making so free with. Old son, says I to myself, why don't you just go and see if perchance those two boyos aren't seeking a sheep ready for the shearing. So I up and followed them outside. I lost them back a ways, but then when I heard you cry out, Captain, I came a'running."

"I'm ever so grateful that you did, Sergeant Pardue," Barclay said as he finished bandaging his arm, took a clean shirt from a closet and put it on.

"You ought to have them brought up before a court-martial. I'll happily testify against them, sir."

"Thank you, Sergeant." Barclay sighed. "Tonight was a call far too close for comfort, I don't mind admitting. I suppose I wouldn't have minded all that much had I lost my money to them—but my life? Ah, that's too high a price to pay."

"You'd not mind losing all that money—eleven thousand dollars, I believe the quartermaster said it was back at the sutler's?"

"Oh, I would rather not lose it, Pardue. But what I meant was that there is a great deal more where it came from."

"And where might that be, Captain, if I may make so bold to ask?"

"In the Superstition Mountains. I'm going back there. Yes, I'm going back there, and you, Sergeant Pardue, are going with me!"

"Me, sir?"

"I said before I didn't know how to repay you for what you did for me tonight. I was wrong. I do know how to repay you. You shall share in my bonanza as a reward for saving my life."

"I didn't butt my big nose into the fracas you got caught up in for a reward. It just seemed like the decent thing to do, is all."

"And most decent of you to it, Pardue. But you won't turn up your 'big nose,' as you call it, at a chance to become a rich man, would you?"

"No, Captain, I don't think I'll choose to do that. But there is one thing."

"What is that, may I ask?"

"I've heard it said that the hidden gold up there in the Superstitions belongs to the Apache thunder gods, or so, at any rate, do the Indians believe. Do you think these heathen thunder gods will take kindly to us trying to steal some of their treasure?"

Barclay chuckled. "We'll try to take it when they're not looking. Now then, Sergeant, can you get off duty long enough to scout the Superstitions with me?"

"I have some leave time coming to me which I can take when I please."

"We could leave tomorrow then. Does that suit you?"

"It does, sir."

"So be it, then. Tomorrow we will set out on our road to riches."

"There's just one more thing, Captain."

"Yes?"

"I'd like to suggest that we split the expenses of our little venture fifty-fifty, if that's all right with you. You see, sir, I'm a man who likes to pay my own way."

"That's fine with me."

When Barclay awoke early the next morning, he found that he was alone in the bed he shared with his wife. He could hear Eva moving about in the main room of the house.

He groaned as he got up because his body and throat were sore and the knife wound in his arm throbbed painfully.

But he ignored his discomfort, preferring to concentrate instead on the days that lay ahead and the good fortune he was sure they held. He was whistling cheerfully when he went into the main room of the house.

But his spirits sank when he saw that Eva was busily packing some of her clothes into a large satchel.

"What are you doing?" he asked her.

"Packing," she answered.

"Yes, I can see that. But why?"

Eva stopped what she was doing and turned to face him. "I'm leaving, Ralph."

"Leaving?"

"I think it's best that I go. Our life together here is just not working out. A large part of the blame is mine," Eva admitted.

"I've never been able to get used to army life or to being an army wife. I've also never been able to get used to living here in Arizona Territory. I've been unhappy, Ralph, and I know you have been, too."

"Eva, we can get through the difficulties we've been having. I'm sure we can. And it's only for another year."

Eva resumed her packing.

"I swore an oath of allegiance, Eva. I have a duty to honor it. What would you have me do? Desert?"

"No, of course not."

"You saw what happened to Corporal Livingston, who deserted last month. When they caught him and brought him back here, he was made to wear a ball and chain for nearly three weeks."

"Another example of the brutality of the army and of life on this post," Eva remarked, stuffing skirts and blouses into her satchel. "But I have said I don't want you to desert. As you said, you have a duty to perform."

"I think that is part of our problem, Eva. You lack a sense of responsibility, of duty."

Eva spun around, her eyes alive with a hot light. "You dare to accuse me of having no sense of duty! I have kept your house diligently. I have stood by your side at official gatherings and said the proper things at the proper times to the proper people. I have honored my marriage commitments in your bed."

"*Our* bed!" Barclay interjected angrily. "But that commitment has been honored more in the breach, as Hamlet might say, than in the observance of late."

"All right, I admit it! Yes, I have turned away from you, just as I have turned away from the unbearable life here in this awful place. You belong to this place, Ralph, and to the army. You certainly don't belong to me anymore. How can you expect me to love a man who is a walking collection of platitudes? Duty. Honor. I am sick to the death of all of it!"

"Duty and honor are not mere platitudes, I will have you know. They are very real to me. They are virtues, Eva, *virtues*."

"No more, Ralph!" Eva cried, covering her face with her hands and beginning to cry. "Please. No more." She struggled for control and then said stiffly, "See what has become of us? We hurl accusations at one another as if were each other's judges. Will it be threats next, Ralph? Will we begin to behave toward each other like bullies in a schoolyard? Oh, Ralph, don't you see what is happening to us?"

"It doesn't have to happen. It never did have to happen."

"Ralph, you are far from blameless in the matter. Army life has begun to brutalize you. You have begun taking me for granted these past months. You have been using me, not loving me."

Stunned by Eva's accusations, Barclay could not utter a sound.

"Now you say you are going off into the wilderness to search for gold," she continued. "You may never find any gold. You may be killed. Do you expect me to simply wait here for the troopers to bring you back draped over your saddle, your scalp gone and arrows in your body?"

"As my wife, it is your duty to—"

"*Duty!*" Eva contemptuously spat the word into the air between them and returned to her packing.

"I am going to search for the gold not for myself alone, Eva, but for both of us. To insure our future together."

Eva straightened. She stood stiffly, but when she spoke again, her voice was sad. "Ralph, our future together does not depend upon gold. At least, it never did in years past. We had each other.

"Now the gold is a way of filling up the emptiness you feel inside because of the way things have been between us of late. You think the gold will recover our old happiness. It won't Ralph. Believe me, it won't any more than returning to Boston will bring me the happiness I also have lost."

Barclay took a step backward and braced himself to say what he felt compelled to say. "I think you have made a wise decision, Eva. I think it is best for both of us if you leave. Are there arrangements to be made?"

"I shall make them. I plan to leave here this Thursday and travel to Phoenix, where I will take the eastbound stage."

"Very well."

Silence invaded the house as Barclay washed and dressed and Eva continued packing her clothes.

Barclay and Pardue rode into Phoenix that night. Both of them were armed. Barclay had a standard-issue single-action Army Colt in his waistband and a Winchester .44-caliber carbine in his saddle boot. Pardue also packed an Army Colt, but the long gun he carried in his saddle boot, though a .44 caliber like Barclay's, held seventeen rounds, four more than Barclay's carbine, and its barrel measured twenty-four inches, four more than Barclay's weapon.

They found the town wide awake and alive with action. Piano music drifted out into the darkness from a saloon. From another saloon across the street came the sound of a woman singing to the accompaniment of a hurdy-gurdy. In the distance a shot rang out. It was followed by the raucous barking of several unseen dogs.

The boardwalks on both sides of the street were crowded with pedestrians, and the street was full of careening wagons and men on horseback. The town's business establishments were all open and doing what Pardue called "a land-office business" by lamplight.

The humid air was stirred by a sluggish breeze coming from the direction of the nearby Salt River.

"What's first on the agenda, Captain?" Pardue asked as they rode around a wagon that sat stranded in the middle of the street while its driver tried alternately to calm his team and repair his broken axle.

"The livery stable," Barclay answered, pointing to the building in front of which several men sat smoking and whittling on cracker barrels and produce crates.

They rode up to the building, drew rein, and dismounted. After wrapping the reins of their mounts around a hitch rail in front of the livery, they went inside to find the hostler shoveling manure out of an empty stall.

"We'd like to buy a mule," Barclay told the man.

"Out back in the corral. There's a half-dozen or so of them. Take your pick. Need a horse, too? Got a few fine ones out back I can let you have cheap."

"Just the mule," Barclay said and went out through the back door of the livery to examine the mules that shared a corral with several horses.

"Swaybacked, most of them," Pardue observed, "though that jet-black one looks like he might carry a load without his legs giving out on him." Pardue went into the corral, pulled back the lips of the mule he had singled out, and then returned to Barclay. "He's a year old, two at the most."

Pardue went to the door of the livery and called out to the hostler, "What'll it take for you to part with the mule that's black as the devil's heart?"

"Fifteen dollars," the hostler called back.

"We'll give you five," Pardue told him.

"He's worth twenty if he's worth a penny."

"Six. That's our best offer. Take it or leave it."

"Seven."

"Six-fifty," Pardue offered, "and at that price this deal is nothing short of highway robbery."

"Done," said the hostler.

After doing business at the livery stable, they bought feed for the mule and the horses and arranged to board their mounts overnight.

Their next stop was at a hotel farther down the street, where they rented a room for the night.

Two hours later their room was packed with the supplies and equipment they had bought at the general store around the corner. The goods included a pack saddle, a raw sheepskin, saddle pad, lengths of canvas and rope, cooking utensils, provisions, and picks, shovels and a nine-pound sledge.

When they had accumulated all they needed for the trip ahead, it took each of them three trips back to the hotel to stow the gear in their room.

After their final trip, Pardue sat down heavily on the bed in the room, took off his hat, and wiped the sweat from his face with the back of his hand. "I'm so hungry my belly's taken to thinking my gullet's been cut. What say we head for that restaurant across the street, Captain?"

They left the hotel and made their way to the restaurant, which bore a sign in its window that said: HOME COOKED MEALS.

Once inside, Pardue looked around. "Place looks none too clean. Captain, you think they serve food here that might not poison a man?"

"We'll find out soon enough, Ben," Barclay said, sitting down at a table near the door.

They ordered the day's special, which the waiter described as fried beefsteak, baked potatoes, boiled string beans, all the bread and butter you can eat, and all the coffee you can drink for just eight bits."

"Not bad," pronounced Pardue some time later as he sopped up the bloody juices from his beefsteak with a piece of brown bread. "I've had worse."

When Barclay said nothing, Pardue gave him an appraising look and asked, "Something bothering you, Captain?"

Barclay, distracted by his own thoughts of Eva and her impending departure from Fort McDowell, did not hear the question but did hear it when Pardue reached out, gripped his arm, and repeated the query.

"Sorry, Ben," he said. "I was lost in thought. Yes, I suppose you could say something is wrong. My wife is going to leave me three days from now—on Thursday."

"Ah, now, it's sorry I am to hear that, Captain."

Barclay shrugged. "It may be for the best. We haven't been getting along lately. Army life doesn't agree with Eva. She's going home to Boston. Maybe it's a blessing in disguise."

"What makes you say that?"

"Lately we've been at each other's throats like two bulldogs. If we separate temporarily, maybe things will be better between us."

"She means to wait on you back there in Boston, is that it?"

The question unnerved Barclay, not only because he didn't know how to answer it, but also because he had never, until now, considered the possibility that he and Eva would not be reunited at some time in the future. But she had not even suggested that such would be the case. Nor, he realized with a sinking feeling, had he.

His body suddenly grew tense. A muscle in his jaw jumped. Pardue suggested that they go to one of the saloons in town and have a drink. "You look like you could use one," he told Barclay. "When a man's wife leaves him, there's not a whole helluva lot he can do except have a drink either to celebrate the joyous occasion or to drown his sorrows in the face of the disaster her leaving means to him."

The saloon Barclay and Pardue chose, the Arizona, was crowded with men and a few women. Every table in the place was occupied. They shouldered their way through the mob and found a place for themselves at the bar.

"Whiskey," Pardue told the barkeep and turned to Barclay, who ordered the same.

"To success," said Pardue, raising his glass.

Barclay, his glass clinking against Pardue's, repeated, "To success."

Near the bar a piano player brought his instrument to life, and as he did a man rose from a table, seized the wrist of a woman who had been sitting at the table with him and two other men, and practically dragged her into the middle of the room. He began to dance with her in a space not much bigger than a saddle blanket, his right arm holding her close while his left hand chucked her under the chin.

"Pretty as a picture," Pardue commented appreciatively, his eyes on the woman.

Barclay glanced at her and then looked down at his drink as if he expected to find the answer to his marital problems floating in the amber liquid.

The dancing man stomped wildly about in the small space, twirling the woman around and around while he sang the words of the song the piano player was pounding out at the top of his coarse voice.

He was a heavyset man with thick lips and eyebrows as big as small bushes. Sweat gleamed on his forehead and dampened the hair on his chest, which was visible in the *V* of his partially unbuttoned shirt.

The woman he was holding kept turning her head from side to side in an effort to escape the probing finger under her chin.

She was a woman of average height who looked between twenty and twenty-five years of age. Despite her grim expression, there was a look of injured innocence about her. She had applied entirely too much powder to whiten the skin of her face and rouge to accentuate her pert lips.

Her hair was a mass of blond curls, some of which had been pasted to her forehead with saliva. Her brown eyes flashed in fury as the finger of the man she was dancing with probed, not her chin, but the cleavage revealed by her yellow silk dress, which had a tear in its hem and a seam that had split under her right arm.

"Look at her, Captain," Pardue said, nudging Barclay with his elbow. "I'm willing to wager she's one who could give a man a pretty good run for his money."

Barclay glanced at the woman. Her body, he noted, was not buxom, but it was attractive. As he watched her, he felt desire stir within him, and then a vague sense of guilt.

But Eva was leaving him, wasn't she? He was a normal man with normal desires. He couldn't be expected to live the life of a monk, when his bed had been forsaken by the woman he had married.

The music stopped.

So did the dancing.

The woman Barclay was watching tried to pull away from the man she had been dancing with. He wouldn't let her go. He began to pull her through the crowd toward a door in the rear of the room. She struggled, digging in her heels.

He merely laughed and pulled harder. She was dragged across

the floor, falling to her knees at one point. The man continued to drag her through the sawdust covering the floor.

She managed to regain her feet. The instant she did, she swung her free left hand in a wide arc. Her hand struck the man full in the face.

The sound of her slap caused some of the men in the room to laugh uproariously. One of them called out to the man she had just struck.

"You got yourself a real wild woman there, Bixby. Hang on to the hellcat!"

Pardue guffawed and ordered another drink. "Who do you put your money on, Captain? The hellcat or her customer? Me, I'll take the customer. He's got a good hundred pounds on her."

Barclay was about to respond when his attention was diverted by the two men who had been sitting at the table with the woman and the man she had just slapped. The older and taller of the two men leaped to his feet and fought his way through the crowd.

When he reached the woman, he backhanded her, reddening her cheek.

Barclay could see his lips moving, but he couldn't hear what the man was saying. He saw him point at the woman, then at the man named Bixby who was still gripping her wrist, and then at the door behind them.

Barclay rose and pushed through the crowd.

"Captain, you're heading for trouble," Pardue called out, but Barclay didn't answer him.

By the time he reached the woman and the two men, he was struggling to control his temper.

"The lady doesn't like your company," he said stonily to Bixby, who was trying once more to drag the woman away. "Let her go."

"Mind your own business, mister!" Bixby snapped.

"Let her go," Barclay said a second time.

When Bixby didn't, Barclay let his fist fly. It caught Bixby on the chin, snapping his head to one side and causing him to release his hold on the woman, who stepped backward as if to get out of harm's way.

"Why you interfering son of a bitch—"

Before Bixby could swing on him, Barclay buried his left fist in Bixby's gut.

Then, when he felt someone seize him from behind, he shook himself free, spun around, and found himself confronting the man who had just backhanded the woman.

As the man suddenly lunged for him, Barclay let him have a right hook, then a left jab while ignoring the pain in his wounded arm that his actions caused him.

The man went down. He lay on the dirty floor, then propped himself up on his elbows and, to Barclay's immense surprise, began to grin.

"Need some help, Captain?"

Out of the corner of his eye, Barclay could see Pardue standing next to him. "Not this time, Ben. This time I'm sober. I was on the boxing team at Harvard University."

"Let's take him, the both of us," Bixby snarled as he helped the other man to his feet.

"Let it be, Bixby," the man said, still grinning. To Barclay, he said, "I admire a man who's good with his fists, sir. Please allow me to introduce myself. My names is Chase Ransom." He held out his hand.

Barclay hesitated a moment and then shook it. "Ralph Barclay."

"Pleased to make your acquaintance, Barclay. Now can you tell me why you have interfered with Betsy's tête-à-tête with Mr. Bixby?"

"I don't see what business that is of yours, Mr. Ransom."

"Oh, it's very much my business. You see, Betsy here works for me."

Barclay glanced at Betsy, who met his gaze with a defiant stare. "I see," he said, turning back to Ransom. "What has Mr. Bixby paid you for the pleasure of her company?"

"Ten dollars."

Barclay's attention was drawn to the younger man who had been at the table and now had taken up a position by Chase Ransom's side.

"You want I should bounce him about a bit, Chase?" the newcomer asked. "I'm game."

"This is my younger brother, Willy," Chase said pleasantly. "He has the mistaken notion that he has to look out for his older brother's well-being." Turning to Willy, Chase said, "We're talking business, boy. Don't interrupt."

"I was just—"

Chase cocked his head to one side and held up a hand.

Willy said nothing more.

Chase turned back to Barclay. "Now then, where were we?"

"Twenty dollars," Barclay said.

Pardue, beside him, whistled softly through his teeth.

Betsy, her eyes on Barclay, patted her spit curls.

"Twenty dollars," Chase repeated. Then he nodded. "You want to top Barclay's offer, Bixby?" he asked.

Bixby snorted. "She's not worth ten, never mind twenty. I'll have my money back, if you don't mind." After Chase handed Bixby a gold eagle, he stalked off.

"Payment in advance," said a beaming Chase, holding out his hand to Barclay, who dug into his pocket and handed the man a twenty-dollar bill.

Chase looked at it and frowned at Barclay.

"It's good," Barclay assured him.

"Not for its face value, it isn't," Chase countered. "Out here on the frontier, most places don't give you full value for paper money. They discount it, as you no doubt know, by as much as forty percent. You wouldn't happen to have any hard money on you, would you? Any gold?"

Barclay and Pardue exchanged glances. "Not at the moment," Barclay said, and Pardue smiled.

The doctor handed Chase an additional five-dollar bill. "Will that do?"

"It will do just fine," Chase assured him, pocketing the

money. Turning to Betsy, he said, "Don't just stand there, my dear. Take your gentleman friend in the back and show him a real good time, hear?"

Betsy reached out and took Barclay's hand. Without a word, she led him through the door at the rear of the room and into the crudely furnished bedroom beyond, where a lighted lamp glowed faintly.

Chapter Six

"I'm sorry," Barclay murmured less than twenty minutes after he had entered the dirty bedroom with the woman named Betsy. "I don't know what's the matter with me. This has never happened before."

Betsy sat up in the bed they shared and looked down at Barclay, who was lying on his back, his arms placed stiffly at his sides, his eyes closed. "It doesn't matter, you know," she told him offhandedly.

Barclay opened his eyes and looked up at her. "I don't want you to think it has anything to do with you. Really, it doesn't"

Betsy put out a hand and gently patted his face.

Barclay reached up and covered her hand with his own.

"You're married, aren't you?" she asked.

"Yes."

"I thought so."

"Did you?" He wondered what she meant.

"You haven't been married long, though, have you?"

"Why, no, not long. What are you, Betsy, psychic?"

She threw her head back and began to laugh, her blond curls bouncing gaily.

Then, sobering, she withdrew her hand and said, "It doesn't take a stargazer to figure you out. It's happened to me before. Men come to me and some of them, the young married ones like you, well, they can't always manage it and you'd think from the way they go on that it was the end of the world. It isn't, you know."

Betsy got up and began to dress, the lamplight softening her face. "Some of the ones who have a problem are married, like I said. They've had a spat with the wife and so they come with me out of spite, only they don't even know that themselves. Then, when it comes right down to it—no good. They leave like curs someone has taken a stick to. But it's all the same to me, really. They pay whether they get what they paid for or not."

"I didn't come with you to spite my wife."

"You came because you felt sorry for me. You wanted to stop Chase from abusing me."

"Why, yes. I didn't realize you knew."

"I know a lot more than you might think I know. Especially about men. Lord knows, I've been with enough of them. I ought to have learned something about them by this time."

Betsy bent over to smooth her stockings. "What you did was very nice. It's maybe the nicest thing a man ever did for me. Oh, men have given me presents—even a diamond brooch one time. But no one ever tried to protect me before. I know I'll remember it long after I've forgotten your name and what you look like."

"Why do you put up with Chase? You ought to leave him."

Betsy shrugged. "A girl has to earn a living, and in this business you soon learn to take the bad with the good."

"You could get a job somewhere. You could wait on tables, or work in a hotel as a chambermaid. There are all sorts of ways to earn a living. You don't have to—"

Betsy sat down on the bed beside Barclay. "Listen, don't lecture me, all right? Your twenty-five dollars doesn't buy you the right to play preacher with me. Sure, I could get a job in some hash house and let the men feel my bottom and pinch my breasts. They would cozy up to me just the way they do now. Or you said I could make beds in a hotel. Now isn't that just every girl's dream of getting on in this world? Making other people's beds and getting on good terms with the fleas and the bedbugs? You must think I don't have a bit of ambition, but I'm here to tell you that I do have ambition, a whole lot of it. Someday Betsy Whitcomb is going to be *somebody!*"

Barclay smiled.

"Chase isn't so bad," Betsy continued, propping an elbow on a knee and resting her chin in the palm of her hand. "He looks after me to a fare-thee-well, Chase does. He's sort of my protector, and a woman alone on the frontier needs somebody to protect her if she wants to stay safe and sound. Chase has floored more than one man who tried to mess with me. Besides, he's the best I've ever had in bed and not the least bit strange like— Well, never mind about that.

"Chase put one man in the hospital over in Austin, Texas, when the loony came after me with a knife. Chase is real strong. He's not a man you want to tangle with. His brother—you saw him tonight—his name's Willy. I sometimes call him Wee Willy 'cause it gives him proper fits, it does. He's only fifteen years of age, and he has a whole book full of things yet to learn."

Betsy shook with laughter. "Willy's as bad as Chase in some ways, worse in others. That's because first of all he's not the brightest boy in the world and, second of all, because of the way Chase eggs him on to do things I swear Willy would never have thought of doing in a whole month of Sundays if left to himself. The Ransoms are from Arkansas—up there in the Ozark Mountains. Chase has gotten rid of most of the rough edges he had when I first hooked up with him in Fort Smith last year. He's a quick learner, Chase is. He watches people real close—how they talk, how they walk. Then he imitates them. Sometimes he even fools me into thinking he was born with a silver spoon in his mouth. But then I listen to Willy, who sounds like a hillbilly for certain, and I remember that Chase is just like Willy except he's got a good disguise. Willy ought to go on back home before Chase turns him into something he'll find out too late he doesn't want to be."

"It sounds to me as if you think Chase is a bad influence on his younger brother."

"He is, for certain. He's taught Willy to lift a purse out of a man's pocket without the man even knowing Willy was ever in the same room with him. Willy should have stayed back home in the hills instead of traipsin' all the way out here hunting his brother, which he did on account of he has the mistaken notion that the sun rises and sets on Chase."

Barclay sat up and swung his legs over the side of the bed. "I'd better get dressed and get going."

"You live here in Phoenix, do you?"

"No. Actually, I'm a doctor stationed with the army at Fort McDowell."

"You're a doctor?" Betsy exclaimed. "I never met a doctor before—in the way of business, I mean. What are you doing in town, Doc?"

"I'm on my way to the Superstition Mountains with a friend. You probably saw him with me tonight."

"That big fellow that was as broad as a barn? The one with the beard?"

"That's him. His name's Ben Pardue."

"What are you two going to do up in the Superstitions? Trap or hunt?"

"Hunt." Barclay hesitated. He glanced at Betsy and then added, "For gold."

"Is that a true fact?"

Barclay, standing up and stepping into his trousers, nodded.

"I've heard talk about there being a whole lot of lost gold somewhere up in the Superstitions. So you and your friend aim to get yourselves some of it, Doc?"

"I already did get myself some. That's why I'm going back for more—if I can find the spot where the gold is located."

"You don't think you can find it again?"

"Oh, I'm sure I can. But when I was taken to the spot, I was blindfolded along the way."

"Blindfolded?"

Barclay, as he buttoned his trousers, told Betsy about being taken to the site of the gold by Chunz and about the legend of the Apache thunder gods who were the supposed owners of the gold while the Apaches were merely the gold's guardians.

"Those thunder gods sound scarier than haunts," Betsy remarked with a shiver.

"They unnerved my wife, too, when I told her about them and about finding the gold and about the things I'd learned during my journey into the mountains while I was blindfolded—"

"What things?"

"Oh, the lay of the land as revealed by the way my horse walked. How long, in my estimation, it took us to get where we were going.

"I even told her what the area looked like where the vein was located, which I could see, of course, once the blindfold was removed. I told her about the trees and bushes and what the mountains looked like, but she wasn't at all impressed."

Betsy rose and slowly crossed the room, then, as slowly, she retraced her steps. "You said before you thought I ought to cut Chase loose. Well, Doc, I'll tell you something. I would if I had something better to latch on to. Now, the way I see it, you could be that something better I've had in mind for a long time."

When Barclay gave Betsy a puzzled glance, she continued, "Take me with you. Look, before you say no, feel my arms. Here, feel." Betsy crooked her arm and placed Barclay's hand on her biceps. "I'm strong. I can dig for gold along with the best of men. I won't be in your way. And I'll only take a quarter of any gold we find. It should be enough for me to get off on my own and start a brand-new life away from Chase. Someplace where nobody knows me and I can start all over fresh."

Barclay, about to reject Betsy's proposition out of hand, hesitated. What would be wrong with taking her along on the quest, he asked himself. He'd paid good money to help her out of a scrape tonight. Why not go whole hog and help her gather a stake that would buy her a ticket to a new life without any excess baggage to burden her like Chase Ransom, who might some day kill her in a fit of fury?

"What do you say, Doc? I can give Chase the slip, and you and me and your friend could be on our way. Oh, it's the chance of a lifetime for me, don't you see? It's the kind of chance I've been waiting for all my life. You're not going to take it away from me, are you?"

"I thought you rather liked your arrangement with Chase."

"Forget about Chase. He's not important. What you've been telling me is. Like I said, I'll give Chase the slip and throw in with you and your friend." Betsy gave Barclay a sly smile. "You won't regret it, either of you. I can be sweet as sugar to men who give me a break."

"You're welcome to come with Ben and me," Barclay said. "But I feel I should warn you. The trip might prove rather rigorous. We'll be camping out in all kinds of weather. We—"

"Did I tell you I can cook a backwoods breakfast over an open fire that would make your mouth water? And not just breakfast. Dinner and supper, too."

"We're leaving in the morning, first light."

"I'll be ready. Where shall we meet?"

"The livery stable. You'll need a horse."

"I've already got a horse. Chase and Willy and me rode in here a month ago. I'll be there at the livery before the first cock crows tomorrow morning. You can count on it!"

"How was it?" Pardue asked Barclay early the next morning as both men set about washing and dressing in the hotel room where they had spent the night.

"How was what?"

"Come now, Captain, you don't want to play coy with me. How was the hellcat? Was she a good hump?"

64

"She's coming with us," Barclay said instead of answering the question.

Pardue stopped scrubbing his face with a washcloth and raised his head. Water dripped from his wet hair and beard as he stared incredulously at Barclay, who was pulling on his boots. "Tell me I'm having ear trouble, Captain. Tell me I couldn't possibly have heard you right."

Barclay looked up at him. "You heard me right. I happened to mention where we were headed and why, and Betsy—her full name is Betsy Whitcomb—expressed an interest in accompanying us. I told her she would be welcome."

"I take it it didn't occur to you to ask my opinion of the matter?"

"Frankly, Ben, it didn't. I didn't think you'd mind having Betsy along. *Do* you mind having her with us?"

"Let me put it to you this way, Captain. I'm not what you could call overjoyed about it. That whore has probably told every man she's ever rassled with between the sheets about our gold by now."

"Our" gold? Barclay made no comment, even though he thought of the vein as *his* gold.

"What's more," Pardue said, using a towel to soak up the water from his hair and beard, "she'll be no help to us. She'll be nothing but a hindrance. There's mountain lions where we're going, not to mention Apaches on the prowl. Letting a woman—especially a woman like her whose only notion of danger is getting caught out by a man whose purse she's lifted—come along is sheer folly, and I don't mind telling you so, Captain."

"Between the two of us, Ben, I'm sure we can look after her."

"I'm in no mood to wet-nurse a woman. Nor am I happy that you have single-handedly taken it upon yourself to reduce my share of our gold"—there it was again: "our" gold—"so that now I only get one-third of the spoils instead of the one-half you agreed would be my share."

"There will be more than enough gold for the three of us. But if you think I've wronged you, Ben, I'm perfectly willing to stick to the original plan. You get half of whatever gold we find, and I'll split my half with Betsy."

Pardue stared at Barclay with an amazed expression on his face. He stopped toweling his hair and beard and said, "You'd really do that for me, Captain?" When Barclay nodded, Pardue clucked his tongue against the roof of his mouth for a moment and said, "You're a most generous man, Captain, I have to say that for you."

"I owe you a debt," Barclay reminded the sergeant. "I mean to see it paid in a fair and equitable manner."

Minutes later both men left the room, carrying some of the gear and provisions they had bought the previous evening. After leaving their loads at the livery, they each made two more trips to collect all their belongings, and then they checked out of the hotel, splitting the bill fifty-fifty, as they had all other expenses.

Later in the livery, Pardue proceeded to show Barclay the proper way to pack a mule.

"First, Captain, comes the *salea*. That's the Mexican name for this here sheepskin. You put it on your mule to keep the load from galling the beast's back. Next the *xerga*."

As Pardue placed the hay-packed square saddle pad over the *salea* and adjusted it so that it hung down to cover both of the mule's sides, Barclay said, "I didn't know you spoke Spanish, Ben."

"I don't really, but I picked up some Mex lingo from when I was stationed down at Fort Ringgold on the Texas border. We used mules a lot to carry gear and provisions down there when we went out after the Mexicans or the Apaches. I truly don't know which set of rascals was worse. The Mexicans would cut your throat as quick as look at you, and the Apaches would take your hair before you even knew they were there.

"Next comes the *aparejo*," Pardue said, hoisting the pack saddle onto the mule's back and then fastening it in place.

"Here, let me help you," Barclay said as Pardue began to wrap their belongings in canvas and pack them on the mule's saddle.

They soon worked out a system: Barclay wrapped and Pardue packed.

"Hold it, Captain!"

"What's wrong?"

"Hold that pack steady, if you will. This foxy little critter's gone and put one over on me. Look there at his saddle girth."

"It's loose," Barclay observed. "How come? I'm sure I saw you tighten it."

Pardue slapped the rump of the mule, which brayed in protest. "He pulled a fast one on me. I should have watched him a bit better. The reason the saddle girth's come loose on him is he sucked in as much wind as he could while I was tightening it."

Pardue bent and began to tighten the girth again. "He thinks he's so almighty smart I ought to let him go the way he was, with the girth practically hanging down to his knees. If I had he would have found out before long that he would be chafed and bruised bad by the load because of his little trick." Pardue straightened up. "Well, that should do it. Now we only have to get our horses ready and we can ride."

"When Betsy gets here."

Pardue muttered something under his breath and went over to where his horse was stalled.

"Doc."

Barclay turned at the sound of Betsy's voice and saw her standing in the open doorway of the stable. The sun was behind her so he could not see her face.

"We've been expecting you," he said. "Are you all set?"

"Yeah, I'm all set. As set as I'm going to be, I guess."

Barclay was conscious of the difference in the sound of her voice. Last night it had been bright and eager. Now it sounded dull.

He went over to her and said, "Didn't you sleep well?"

"No. I was too excited thinking about what's ahead for us."

"Do you feel up to making the journey?"

"I'll manage."

"Let's get our horses. Have you any luggage?"

"A satchel. Chase is bringing it."

"He's coming to see you off?" Barclay asked, surprised.

"No, he's coming with us. Him and Willy are."

Barclay, taken aback by Betsy's announcement, was momentarily at a loss for words. But then, finding his voice, he said, "You shouldn't have told him where you were going. We don't want him and his brother along. I've already had problems with Ben Pardue. He didn't want you to come with us because he didn't want to split the gold three ways. He certainly won't want to split it five ways."

Betsy moved into the barn. As she did so, Barclay was able to see the puffy flesh under her left eye that had begun to turn purplish.

"I didn't invite Chase and Willy to come with us," Betsy told him in a strained tone. "He caught me sneaking out of my room this morning. I told him I couldn't sleep and was going out to get an early breakfast. He knew I was lying because I usually don't get up until noon or later. He started asking me questions. I got so nervous I kept changing my story and he kept getting more and more suspicious. Finally he hit me. Here." Betsy gingerly touched her injured eye. "I'm sorry, Doc. I tried to give him the slip. Honest, I did."

"But it didn't work, did it, Betsy, my dear?" said a smiling Chase Ransom as he appeared in the doorway of the livery with his brother.

Both men, Barclay noted, were now armed. Chase had a Remington revolver hanging from his cartridge belt, and Willy had a Colt Peacemaker in the waistband of his trousers.

"Has she told you, Doctor," Chase said, "that you're to have the pleasure of our company on your gold-seeking expedition?"

"She told me what you did to her, Chase, and I'm telling you that you're not coming with us. This is a strictly private party, and you're not invited."

"I've invited myself, Barclay," Chase shot back. "Now, I asked you politely not to get any notions about trying to stop

Willy and me from joining forces with you. If you try anything—"

"Me and Chase might just decide to let light through you," Willy interrupted, his hand on the butt of his gun and a smirk on his face.

Before Barclay could express the rage he was feeling, Pardue came over and gave him a questioning glance. "What the hell is this crowd doing here?" he asked angrily.

"Chase tells me he and his brother are coming with us," Barclay answered.

"Like hell you are!" Pardue bellowed. "Two's company, five's a mob. Come on, Captain, let's vamoose."

"Ben, wait a minute," Barclay said, then hurriedly explained the situation to Pardue.

"You've gone and got us into one helluva mess, Captain," Pardue shouted. "You and your bighearted invitation to that slut there. She's probably lying to you about getting caught sneaking out of the hotel. Hell, she probably went and told her pimp and his sidekick brother there all about our deal, and here they all are, ready and able and willing to bleed us dry."

"I'm not lying about this," Betsy snapped, vigor in her voice for the first time since she arrived at the livery. She touched the rapidly darkening bruise that was blackening her eye.

"You probably got that from one of your fancy Dan customers," Pardue snarled.

"Calm down, Ben," Barclay urged. "We're going to have to let them come along," he said, indicating the Ransom brothers. "It appears that we have no choice in the matter."

"Now, why would you want to go and say a thing like that, Captain? Sure, we got ourselves a choice in the matter. I'm a fast-draw man, a sharpshooter from way back. Should Chase try to shoot me, I'll drill him first." Pardue spun around so that he was facing Chase. "Like this," he said, his gun quickly clearing leather.

Chase's gun also cleared leather—a crucial instant sooner than Pardue's. It was aimed straight at the sergeant's heart.

"Have I made my point, soldier?" Chase asked Pardue in a silken voice.

Pardue answered the question by sullenly holstering his weapon.

Willy giggled. "You're fast, all right," he told Pardue, "but Chase, he's a whole helluva lot faster. You throw down on Chase, he'll fill your belly full of bullets before you can say Arizona stump-jumper."

Chase turned to Barclay. "Does this soldier also know where the gold's to be found?"

Barclay shook his head.

"Then he's of no use to me, or to you either, for that matter. And he's a troublemaker, as we've just seen. He stays here."

"If he doesn't go," Barclay said, "neither do I. I owe Sergeant Pardue a debt. He gets a share of the gold in payment of that debt."

Chase considered Barclay's statement. "Have it your way, doctor. That matter's not worth arguing about. Now to practical matters. I suppose you and Pardue have packed provisions on that mule of yours over there."

"We've packed food, yes."

"Enough for two?"

When Barclay nodded, Chase said with an almost benign smile, "But we're a party of five now." Before Barclay could say anything more, he added, "You'd better buy another mule and enough food to feed the three of us for a while."

Barclay glanced at the grim-visaged Pardue, who was standing beside him, and then went to search for the hostler.

"Hold on, Barclay," Chase called out to him. "There's one other important matter we have to take care of. Willy, get their sidearms and their saddle guns."

"Wait just one minute here!" Pardue protested, but Chase silenced him by aiming his gun at his forehead.

"Drop your gun belts," Willy ordered, and Barclay and Pardue reluctantly did so. Willy picked them up and went to the stall area. He returned carrying only the two men's guns.

"When we pick up our horses from in front of the hotel, Willy," Chase said, "you pack those guns behind my saddle, hear?"

"Sure thing, Chase."

Barclay bought a second mule from the hostler. As he was about to pay for it, Pardue, who was standing beside him, muttered, "Captain, were I you, I wouldn't flash that fat roll of money around so free and easy. That must be just about all the money you got when you cashed in your gold at the fort."

"It is," Barclay said, pocketing most of his money again and hoping that Chase and the others had not seen how much he was carrying.

"Some men—and I count Chase Ransom among them—would kill for that much money," Pardue commented.

Then, under the alert eyes of Chase and Willy, Barclay went to the general store, where he bought and paid for a quantity of food sufficient for three more people. This time he left most of his eleven thousand dollars in his pocket as he paid for what he had bought. Back at the livery stable again, Pardue helped him pack the provisions on the second mule.

It was midmorning when the party of five left Phoenix. Barclay and Pardue rode in front of the others as Chase had ordered and the sergeant trailed their two-mule string.

"Which way do we go?" Chase asked Barclay as they left Phoenix behind them and his brother began a monotonous whistling.

Barclay pointed to the northeast. "We'll follow the Salt River and ford it near Mormon Flat."

"Betsy told me that Indian blindfolded you," Chase said. "So how are you going to decide exactly where to move into the mountains?"

"Betsy has it wrong," Barclay responded. "I wasn't blindfolded until we got to the mountains. I remember where we went in."

"Where's that exactly?" Willy stopped whistling long enough to ask.

"I'll show you."

No more was said by any of the party for some time. The only sound was the wail of Willy Ransom's endless whistling.

Later, at the bend in the river, Willy stopped whistling and pointed to the calm surface of the water, which looked like molten lead under the bright sun.

"Lookee there, Chase! See 'em? There's a whole big flock of salmon just under the surface of the river. Why don't we stop and try to catch some? We could cook and eat 'em and dry any we got left over. I sure do dote on salmon. Ain't no tastier fish flesh on the face of the earth than salmon, if you ask me. And those down there in the river—look how fat and sassy they are. I bet top dollar they weigh thirty, maybe forty pounds apiece. Some of them look to be nigh on to five feet long!"

Chase ignored his brother.

They rode on through level country that was dotted with cactus of various kinds. At times cactus wrens swooped and swirled around them before darting into holes in dead saguaro cactus.

As they rode on with only the relentless sun to watch their progress, Willy gave up whistling and announced, "My mouth's so parched I can't scare up the spit to whistle with."

By noon they had reached Mormon Flat ford. A little while later they forded the river where Barclay and Chunz had forded it earlier.

The mountains loomed in front of them, silent and vaguely forbidding. Mound Mountain, the highest peak in the Superstitions, stood black and stark in the distance, like a huge claw against the sky.

Barclay scanned the countryside ahead of him and to the north, the direction from which he and Chunz had approached the mountains. His eyes roamed over the several canyons that gaped in the side of the mountains as he tried to identify the one through which he and Chunz had ridden into the Superstitions. He frowned, keenly aware of how similar each of the canyons' mouths appeared, with the single exception of one that had a jagged left wall. That one, Barclay was sure, was not it.

He drew rein and sat with his hands folded around his saddle horn, his eyes on the long line of canyons.

"What's holding us up, Chase?" Willy asked his brother.

"What are you waiting for, Doctor?" Chase asked as he rode up beside Barclay. "Where do we go in?"

"I'm not sure, but give me a few minutes. I'll find the spot. You stay here, and I'll ride out and see what I can see."

"Willy," Chase said, "go with the good doctor. See to it that he doesn't try any tricks."

As Barclay moved out, Willy rode along, whistling again, on his right.

They rode past the mouths of three canyons in the next twenty minutes. Which one was it? Barclay asked himself. He remembered that he had seen a quartet of peaks off to the east while waiting to be blindfolded by Chunz at the canyon mouth. There had been a growth of juniper at the canyon's entrance, he recalled. He immediately corrected himself. It had been a growth of scrub pine, not juniper, that he had seen. Or had he been right the first time?

Sweating, he rode back the way he had just come, squinting at the canyons he had already passed once. Scrub pine, he thought, or juniper? Four peaks in the distance. There had been a creek with a tiny waterfall near the canyon's entrance.

He saw no creek, no water at all.

Then he saw the four peaks standing in a stately row in the east. They towered black against the blue sky like the four fingers of a giant's hand thrusting out of the rocky earth.

He drew rein at the mouth of a canyon through which he had spotted the peaks. There was some scrub growing in the area, but it wasn't pine and it wasn't juniper. There was no creek.

"Barclay!"

The doctor didn't turn at the sound of Chase's harsh voice.

"Is that where we go in?" Chase yelled.

Barclay didn't answer. He wasn't at all sure that he was facing the mouth of the canyon he and Chunz had entered earlier.

He looked up at the four peaks, a reassuring sight.

"This way!" he yelled as he rode into the canyon facing him, hoping that the way he was going would indeed lead him to the thunder gods' gold.

Behind him, Willy let out a wild, *"Whooppeeee!"* and then shouted, "Come on, Chase. *Let's go get rich!"*

Chapter Seven

Barclay, with Pardue at his side, rode up through the twisting canyon. The others followed behind him.

"How far do we have to go, Captain?" Pardue asked him.

Barclay was uncertain. "It seemed to me it took Chunz and me nearly two hours to get to the spot," he answered. He continued scanning the countryside as the canyon through which they were riding gradually narrowed and they found themselves traveling through a thick stretch of chaparral.

"Old Lucifer himself must have planted this garden," Pardue grumbled as the chaparral tore at his boots and and trousers.

"Can't we get the hell out of this underbrush?" Chase called out. "It's making my mount's legs bloody."

"Leave him be, Chase," Willy said before Barclay could respond. "If this is the way to the gold, then this is the way I want to go, by God."

If it *is* the way to the gold, Barclay thought, his uncertainty growing. He could just barely see the tops of the four peaks. The sheer walls of the canyon now towered above him, cutting off his view of the land around him.

"I heard someone say," Pardue ventured, "that stockmen used to graze their cattle up here in these mountains. But I don't see how the hell they could ever do that. The only thing I've seen so far that any self-respecting cow would eat is a patch of filigree—pin clover—back a ways. There's not enough grass up here to feed a goose."

"I'm hungry, Chase," Betsy said. "Can't we stop soon and have something to eat?"

"We'll stop before long. I'm hungry, too, not to mention thirsty."

Barclay tried to recall what the trail had been like after Chunz had blindfolded him and they had resumed their journey.

He remembered they had first turned to the right soon after entering the canyon. Then they had turned sharply left. The canyon they were now in had twisted and turned after they had entered it, but he could not now recall in which directions.

At one point during his earlier journey, he had heard the sound of his horse's hooves striking what must have been granite or possibly limestone. Later on they had traversed a sandy area. He had known that because of the way his horse's gait had changed. It had been brisk on solid ground but had grown slower and somewhat unsteady on the sandy stretch.

They had recently passed over some hardpan, but it hadn't been granite. He reminded himself that he wasn't sure he had passed over granite the first time. It could have been limestone. He had been blindfolded and had not seen it. So the fact that they had not traveled across granite this time didn't necessarily prove that they were on the wrong track.

Fifteen minutes later he became aware of a change in the air. It was slightly cooler now because they had begun to ascend higher into the mountains. He felt encouraged because he recalled his horse laboring upward during the first trip.

"There it is!" Willy whooped from the rear. "Look, Chase, there it *is*!"

Barclay saw the deep hole slanting almost vertically down into the earth up ahead. It had been blasted out of solid rock, and the roof over the shaft's entrance was braced with timber uprights on which a wooden crossbeam rested.

"Dismount!" Chase ordered.

"That's not it," Barclay told him. "It wasn't from a mine that I got the gold. It was from a vein running along the side of a ledge, and the gold was embedded in rose quartz."

Chase rode up to him. He reached out and seized the bridle of Barclay's horse, bringing the animal to a halt. "Are you sure you're not trying to trick us, Barclay? This mine looks interesting."

"It's probably played out," Pardue offered. "You can see as plain as day it's not been worked in a good long time."

"You two make quite a pair," Chase said with a sardonic smile. "One lies and the other swears to the lie."

"I'm not lying," Barclay insisted.

"Why don't we stop here?" Betsy said. "Chase, you and Willy can go look down in the mine while the rest of us get something to eat."

"Good idea," Chase said.

"I'll go fetch us some wood we can turn into torches, Chase," Willy volunteered.

Pardue started to untie the packs on one of the mules as Willy went bounding past him in search of wood.

Pardue was removing cooking utensils and some provisions from their packs when Willy returned with two long pieces of pitch pine. He handed one to his brother and kept one for himself.

Chase lighted his, and as Willy was about to do the same, Chase said, "I'll go down. You stay here and keep an eye on things. Make sure nobody goes for those guns I've got packed on my horse."

"Aw, Chase, I was counting on going down into the mine. How come you're always the one who gets to do things and I always have to stay behind?"

"We'll take turns," Chase said. "I'll go first." He gingerly began his descent into the darkness of the mine, which his lighted torch could not entirely dispel.

Pardue took a plug of Winesap tobacco from his pocket and bit off a piece. Chewing vigorously, he spat a stream of brown tobacco juice that just barely missed hitting Willy's boots. He then carried the cooking utensils and provisions he had unpacked over to the smoky fire that Barclay was building.

"That's no way to do it, Captain, if you don't mind my saying so," he commented.

When Barclay looked up at him, Pardue pointed and said, "You've used green wood, Captain. That stuff'll smoke up the whole place and announce to anybody within miles of this spot that we're here. Could be Apaches might see that smoke."

Pardue proceeded to stamp out the fire Barclay had built, and then he dispatched the doctor to find some dry deadwood.

Barclay returned later carrying wood which met with Pardue's approval. The doctor soon had another fire going, this one under some trees so the almost negligible smoke would be lost in the branches.

"There's no use," he had said, "announcing our presence to every Tom, Dick, and Harry who might be in the vicinity. You can never tell who they might be and what they might take it in mind to do to us should they come upon us."

Betsy had stared at Pardue in alarm as he spoke.

"Are there Indians here?" Betsy asked nervously after observing the careful attempt to obscure the fire.

"There could be," Barclay replied.

Betsy glanced uneasily around the shadowy area. Then, as Barclay began to sort through the provisions that Pardue had unpacked, she said, "Here, let me help."

She placed some shortening in a skillet and then, using water from her canteen, washed some rice and placed it in the skillet. She asked Barclay to open two cans of tomatoes.

She peeled and chopped an onion and held the skillet over the fire. When the rice had begun to brown, she added the onion and then the tomatoes, together with their liquid. Using a tin fork, she mashed the tomatoes before adding some salt to the mixture.

Meanwhile, Barclay had put the coffeepot on the fire. He accepted the plate of rice and tomatoes Betsy handed him and proceeded to eat. "Tasty," he told her.

"It's not too salty?" When Barclay shook his head, Betsy said, "When my ma was teaching me how to cook, she always said that I had a real heavy hand when it came to adding salt to things."

She scooped some more of the mixture onto a plate and handed it to Pardue. He said nothing, but merely ate it.

"Wee Willy, you come on over here and get some vittles," Betsy called out.

"Don't call me that!" Willy snapped as he came over to the fire and Betsy filled a plate for him. "I told you never to call me that!"

Betsy flinched in mock fear when Willy raised his hand as if to strike her. "You hit me, Wee Willy," she said, "and I'll turn Chase loose on you. He'll soon teach you to mind your manners."

Willy muttered an oath, took the plate Betsy was holding out to him, and strode away.

When Pardue finished what was on his plate, he took some pieces of dried apple from a cloth bag and used them to sop up the juices left by the tomato-and-rice mixture. Then, putting down his plate, he rose and went over to the canyon wall, where he sat down in the shade with his back against the rock, his hat pulled down over his eyes, and his arms folded across his burly chest.

"Doc," Betsy said, "I'm sorry about what happened. I should have had more sense than to let myself get caught by Chase back there at the hotel."

"That was definitely a bit of bad luck."

Betsy ate a spoonful of food. "I've had a lot of bad luck in my life. Oh, I'm not complaining. I'm just saying what's true. Chase is only the latest bad luck I've had. I wish I'd never gotten mixed up with him."

"When we discussed your relationship with Chase before," Barclay said, "you sounded partial to him."

"Not partial to him. Used to putting up with him, is more like it. Except for the sex, which, with him, is real good, like I said. But him—*he's* no good. Chase Ransom is bad clear through. Not just for any woman he happens to get his hands on, either. He's bad for men, too. But at least men can fight him back."

Barclay studied Betsy as she gazed off into the distance, the food on her plate forgotten. She had a bereft expression on her face. She looked like a child who had lost a treasured plaything.

"I'm so glad I've finally found my chance," Betsy said. "It's a good feeling to know I'm on my way to a new life with no one like Chase to mistreat me anymore. Doc, that gold of yours is going to be my first-class ticket to glory, and I don't mean the kind of heavenly glory preachers hallelujah about, but the kind a rich woman can find right here on earth."

Sometime later, as Barclay sat by the fire drinking a cup of black coffee and listening to a sleeping Pardue snoring in the distance, he saw flames rising from the abandoned mine. Like the fires of hell breaking through to the surface, he thought. And there was one of Satan's own imps, he thought next as Chase emerged from the mine.

"Any luck, Chase?" Willy cried, leaping to his feet and running toward his brother.

"It's played out," Chase answered, dropping his torch and stomping it out. "It was a silver mine. You can still see some silver down there, but not enough to mine anymore. The place is full of water and mud, and the timbers supporting the roof are rotting."

"You sure, Chase?" Willy persisted. "You real sure the mine's played out?" he asked as he accompanied his brother over to the fire, where Chase helped himself to what was left of the rice and tomatoes.

"It's deader'n a doornail," Chase said with disappointment as he hunkered down and began to eat. "Hey, this stuff's cold," he yelled at Betsy, who was standing on the other side of the fire with her arms folded, watching him with a chilly look in her eyes.

Her look grew colder as she said, "You're not crippled, Chase. You want hot food, put it back in the skillet and put the skillet back on the fire."

"Cooking's woman's work!" he barked, holding his plate out to her. When she made no move to take it from him, he rose and came round the fire.

Shoving his plate at her, he ordered her to warm up the food. Betsy took the plate from him and sullenly scraped its contents into the skillet.

"I'm going down into that mine, Chase," Willy announced.

"What for? I told you it's played out."

"Maybe you missed some silver down there, Chase. Maybe I'll find what you missed."

"Stay put," Chase ordered his brother. "We'll be pulling out of here as soon as I finish eating, which I doubt I'll ever do if Betsy doesn't get a move on with that skillet."

"Here," she snapped and dumped the heated contents of the skillet onto Chase's plate.

Again Chase hunkered down and began to eat. "This stuff's terrible. It's as salty as Lot's wife."

Betsy made no response.

Chase turned to Barclay and said, "I hope your bonanza is richer than that mine down there."

"It is," Barclay assured him.

"It may be," Chase said, tipping his plate and pouring the remaining food into his mouth. "But it won't do us the least bit of good if we don't find it, will it? Are you sure you know where it is?"

"Of course I'm not sure. I was blindfolded when Chunz brought me up here into the mountains."

"You must have spotted some landmarks before and after that savage blindfolded you. You ought to be able to pick them out."

"I'm doing my best."

Chase's eyes narrowed as he gave Barclay an appraising

glance. "Maybe you lied to Betsy. Maybe you made up that story you told her about finding gold up here with the help of some Indian."

"Why would I lie to her?"

"How the hell do I know? Maybe to make yourself seem like a big man in her eyes. Did you lie, Doctor?"

"I didn't lie. The gold is here in the mountains, and I intend to find it."

"What makes you think he lied about finding gold?" Pardue asked as he joined the others around the fire. "That eleven thousand dollars he got for the gold was no lie. Though I didn't see the gold the captain found, I did see the cash money he got for it. So why don't you relax, Chase, and stop worrying so much."

"Let me tell you something, Barclay," Chase said, ignoring Pardue. "You try leading us on a wild-goose chase, you'll never come out of these mountains alive. I'll make damn sure of that!"

A muffled cry followed by the loud sounds of falling rock suddenly filled the air.

"What the hell was that?" a startled Chase asked.

"Look!" Betsy cried, pointing at the thick cloud of dust that was rising from the depths of the mine.

"Where's Willy?" Chase asked, looking around. He swore. "That damn fool's gone. Unless I miss my guess, he went down in that mine after I told him not to. Damn his hide! I'll whip him within an inch of his life when he crawls out of there."

"Maybe you won't get a chance to do that, Chase," Pardue remarked laconically.

"What do you mean?"

"I mean that sounded like a pretty bad cave-in to me. Maybe your brother's buried down there for good."

Chase sprang to his feet and sprinted toward the entrance to the mine. He peered down into it, then picked up the piece of pitch pine he had taken down into the mine earlier and set it afire. Holding the torch high above his head, he started down into the mine.

The others hurried over to the mine's entrance and watched

him descend. They could see his torch flickering far below them and then—nothing.

"He must have turned a corner into a tunnel," Pardue speculated.

"Can you hear anything?"

"I can't hear anything," Betsy said.

"I'm going down to see if I can help," Barclay said. "I'll make myself a torch and be right back."

Betsy grabbed his arm to prevent him from leaving. "Don't go down there. You might get hurt. Besides, this is our chance, don't you see?"

"Chance?"

"With Chase and Willy both down there in the mine, you and Pardue could get your guns back. Then when Chase comes back up, with or without Willy, we would have the upper hand again."

Barclay stared at Betsy in disbelief. "Willy might be badly hurt. I have to go down there and see if I can help."

"Doc, don't—"

Betsy got no further with what she had been about to say, because Chase suddenly reappeared far below them, the torch in his hand.

They watched Chase scramble up the steep slope of the mine shaft. When he stood before them, panting and wiping the sweat from his forehead with the back of his free hand, he said, "Willy's cut off by a rockfall in a tunnel down there. I couldn't get to him."

"Could you hear him?" Betsy asked.

"No."

"He must be dead," she said.

Barclay was shocked by the expression of hope that flared on her face. "We've got to go down and try to dig him out," he said.

"I'll go with you, Captain," Pardue volunteered.

"We'll need torches, picks, and shovels," Barclay said. He went to get them, followed by Pardue.

When they returned several minutes later, Barclay was carrying two long pieces of pitch pine and Pardue was carrying a pick and shovel.

"The three of us can spell each other," Pardue suggested. "Take turns trying to dig Willy out."

"You two will take turns," Chase said. "I'm staying up here."

"But it's your brother down there," Barclay exclaimed. "You mean to say you don't intend to help us try to rescue him?"

"That's exactly what I mean to say."

Barclay suppressed the anger he was feeling and beckoned to Pardue. "Let's go, Ben."

They lit their torches and went, both of them moving cautiously down the steeply slanting shaft of the mine.

"Watch your step," Pardue warned unnecessarily, because Barclay was watching every unsteady step he was taking. "These support timbers don't look any too stable."

"I find it hard to believe," Barclay said as he continued his descent, "that Chase wouldn't come down here to help his own brother."

"I don't, Captain."

When the shaft became a dead end in front of them, they turned into the tunnel that ran at right angles to it. Less than twenty yards ahead, they saw the rockfall that blocked the tunnel.

"He may be buried underneath all those rocks," Barclay remarked. "Or maybe, if he was lucky, he's beyond them and not badly hurt. If he is beyond the rockfall, he might have a chance, depending on whether or not he's able to get enough oxygen to breathe during the time it takes us to get to him. Let's start digging."

Pardue used rocks to brace their torches in an upright position, and then the men began digging with the pick and shovel.

Chapter Eight

"The first thing we had better do is make a hole in this rock barrier," Barclay said. "If Willy is behind it, he'll be using up the available oxygen back there fast. I'll try to get through here while you work that side."

Barclay proceeded to focus his digging efforts on a small area just large enough to make an air passage through to the other side. Several feet away from him Pardue swung the pick over his head and brought it down to shatter several rocks which were wedged tightly together.

Granite dust began to fill the air in the narrow tunnel, and soon both men were coughing from it, but they kept doggedly on. Barclay abandoned the shovel and began digging with his hands, which soon became raw and bloody. Finally he let out a cry of triumph.

"You get through, did you, Captain?" Pardue asked him.

"I did!" Barclay crowed. He thrust his hand into the hole he had made, which was no more than five inches in diameter. His wrist followed his hand. When his arm was in the hole up to his

elbow, he said, "This wall of rock is nearly two feet thick, Ben."
He withdrew his arm.

Pardue's response was a noncommittal grunt.

"Willy!" Barclay called, his mouth at the hole he had made.
"Can you hear me, boy?"

He listened but heard no response.

"He must be under all these rocks, Captain," Pardue said solemnly.

Although he knew that Pardue might be right, Barclay nevertheless picked up the shovel and began to ram it into the rock wall in front of him. Gradually he managed to widen the hole he had made. Bit by bit he continued to enlarge it, working downward to make a passage that he could crawl through.

His and Pardue's shadows capered on the walls as they worked, both of them concentrating now on widening the air hole Barclay had made in the rocky barrier before them. The damp heat in the tunnel wrung sweat from their bodies and the stone dust swirling in the air clogged their nostrils, making it difficult to breathe.

One of the torches burned itself out. Pardue tried relighting it, but the piece of pitch pine had become nothing but charred wood and would not ignite.

They continued working until the hole was a good foot and a half wide and nearly two feet high.

Barclay again called Willy's name. He tried not to think of the all too real possibility that the boy might be lying crushed to death beneath the rockfall.

He didn't know how long he and Pardue had been working to widen the hole that would eventually give them access to the area beyond the rockfall when the tunnel suddenly brightened.

Blinking, Barclay turned to find Chase standing at the spot where the shaft ended and the tunnel began. He felt relief at the sight of the man. He was delighted to discover that Chase had changed his mind and had come down to help, because his arms were aching and his bloody hands kept slipping and sliding on the handle of the shovel he was using to widen the hole.

"You take a turn at it, Chase," Pardue said, slumping down on the ground and dropping his pick. "I'm tuckered."

"Is he back behind there?" Chase asked.

"We don't know," Barclay answered. "He could be. We've broken through so he can get some air if he is."

"He could be under all those rocks," Chase said.

"He could be," Barclay agreed reluctantly.

He was about to resume digging when Chase said, "Let me by."

Chase shouldered Barclay out of the way. Putting his mouth close to the hole, he yelled, "Willy, if you're in there, answer up. You hear?"

He put his ear to the hole. "He doesn't answer," he said, as if he were talking to himself. He called Willy's name a second time.

"Here," Pardue said, offering Chase his pick. "You have at it for a spell."

"We're wasting time," Chase said, ignoring Pardue. "Let's get out of here."

"Chase, you can't be serious!" Barclay exclaimed. "We've got to find Willy."

"What we've got to find, Barclay, is that gold of yours. Now let's get out of here and be on our way."

"Talk about cold-blooded bastards!" Pardue muttered.

"I'm not leaving," Barclay announced. "Not until we find Willy and know for certain whether he's alive or dead."

"Barclay," Chase said, "you're going to do exactly what I tell you to do." He drew his gun and aimed it at the doctor. "Move on out of this mine, both of you."

Pardue, growling something unintelligible, got wearily to his feet and headed for the shaft.

Barclay, behind him, shook his head, his eyes locked on Chase. "I'm not going. I'm going to keep on digging."

Chase cocked his gun.

Barclay lowered his eyes and saw Chase's finger grow taut on the gun's trigger. He looked up and met the man's gaze again. 'If you kill me, Chase, you'll never find the gold."

Chase seemed to ponder the statement. Then he said, "Do you

really think my brother's alive in there?" he asked Barclay as Pardue stood, his eyes flicking back and forth between the two men.

"I don't know. But I'm going to find out."

"It seems you're a man who likes long odds," Chase said sternly. "You know if we leave now, we split any gold we find four, not five ways."

Barclay's contempt for Chase Ransom doubled in that instant, but he said nothing. Instead he began to dig, this time using the pick to break through the rock barrier.

"Look out, Captain!" Pardue called from behind him. "He's going to shoot!"

Barclay didn't have time to react. The sound of Chase's shot in the confined space of the tunnel was like an explosion of dynamite. The bullet embedded itself in the wall to Barclay's right.

He continued digging, his body tense, his mind made up. He would not give in and obey Chase's order to abandon Willy. He would do what he felt he had to do. He would try his best to save Willy.

He wondered when Chase's next shot would come. He was sure the first one had missed its mark deliberately. It had been both a threat and a warning. Would Chase deliberately miss with his second shot or would he—

Pardue joined Barclay and began to dig. "You've got nerves of iron, Captain, I'll say that for you."

"Apparently you have the same, Ben," Barclay said with a thin smile.

"No. Just a lack of good common sense, I reckon."

Minutes later Pardue stopped digging and gripped Barclay's arm. "Did you hear something, Captain? I swear I did."

"What did you hear?"

"I don't know. Something faint. Maybe it was the kid."

They listened, and they both heard it this time. Willy's voice, weak and seeming to come to them from a great distance.

"Chase."

The name was a whisper on the air, the ghost of a sound.

"It's him!" Barclay exulted. He called out, "Willy, hold on! We're going to get you out of there."

He and Pardue dug furiously, attacking the remaining rocks surrounding the hole they made with hopeful gusto. Then Barclay, impatient with their progress, said, "I'm going in."

"You'll never make it, Captain. You'll get stuck for sure."

"If I do, push me through."

A determined Barclay squeezed into the hole they had made. He wriggled, twisting and turning, as he forced himself into the opening, arms first. Ahead of him was darkness. Behind him, silence.

Suddenly he found he could not move a muscle. Panic rioted through him. He struggled to move forward. When that didn't work, he tried to fight his way backward. But he was immobilized, unable to move at all. His skin became clammy. Sweat ran into his eyes.

"Chase? Is that you, Chase?"

The sound of Willy's weak voice gave Barclay the strength he needed to fight down the panic that had seized him. "It's Dr. Barclay, Willy. I'm coming to get you out."

But he knew he was going nowhere. He was totally unable to move. Would Pardue be able to widen the passage in time to save both himself and Willy?

Forget Pardue, he told himself. The good Lord helps them who help themselves. Making a superhuman effort, the blood drumming in his brain, his heart fluttering in his chest, his fingers scrambling for purchase on the rocky surface, he managed to pull himself forward.

"I'm scared, Doc."

"Don't be." Another minuscule move forward. "We're going to get you out of there."

Then, by twisting his feet and bracing them on either side of the passage, Barclay was able to push himself the final few inches into the tunnel beyond the point at which it was blocked. He tumbled down the few feet to the floor of the tunnel.

"Light, Ben!" he yelled at the top of his voice. "Hold your torch up to the opening!"

Faint light filtered into the tunnel, allowing Barclay to see that Willy was lying with his left leg pinned beneath a fallen timber. He crawled on his hands and knees to where the boy lay. As he did so, he noticed the dried blood on the back of Willy's head.

"Are you badly hurt?" he asked when he was kneeling beside the injured boy.

"I don't rightly know, Doc. My head feels like it's on fire, and I think my leg's busted."

Barclay rose and, groaning, removed the timber that had pinned Willy's left leg. When he had freed the limb, he said, "I'm going to check for broken bones. I don't want to hurt you, but I might. You understand?"

"Go ahead, Doc."

Barclay knelt down. His sensitive fingers gently probed Willy's leg. He quickly discovered that the boy's tibia was broken. "Don't move now. Let me have a look at your head. The skin's broken, but I don't think the skull is."

"I was out like a light after one of those rocks hit me on the head, Doc. I don't know how long it was. I didn't wake up till I heard the shooting over on the other side. Who was doing the shooting, Doc?"

"Never mind about that now. We'll have time to talk once I've gotten you out of here. That's something that is going to take some doing, and it may cause you pain. You feel up to it?"

"I don't feel up to spending the rest of my life holed up down here, Doc."

Barclay crawled back to the opening. "Ben!"

"Captain?"

"Ben, try to make the passageway wider if you can. Willy's got a broken leg and I want to make it as easy as possible for him to get through to your side."

"Right you are, Captain!" Pardue said, as he began working at the rockfall again.

As the jarring clang of iron against granite continued, Barclay used his hands and knife to pry away the loose rocks.

"I'll give you a hand, Doc," Willy offered and began to drag himself across the floor of the tunnel to where Barclay was working.

"Only one of us can work in this mouse hole at a time," Barclay told him. "I think it would be best if you were to just sit tight and take it easy."

An hour later Barclay decided that he and Pardue had widened the passageway sufficiently for him and Willy to attempt to ease through it.

"You'll go first, Willy," Barclay said. "I'll bring up the rear." Then calling out to Pardue, he said, "Willy's coming through, Ben. You grab his hands when you can and ease him along. Ready?"

"Ready, Captain."

"Here you go, Willy," Barclay said, helping the boy to stand on his good right leg and then to climb clumsily up and into the passageway. He watched as Willy's body began to disappear little by little.

"I got him!" Pardue's muffled voice announced several minutes later.

When the passageway was empty, Barclay climbed into it, surprised at how easy it was to get through this time.

As he emerged on the other side, the first thing he noticed was that Chase, who was leaning against the tunnel wall, had holstered his revolver. The second thing he noticed was the smile on Willy's face as he gazed up at his brother from where he lay on the floor of the tunnel.

"I guess you thought I was a goner, didn't you, Chase?" Willy asked, shifting position and wincing in pain.

"You're one damn fool, Willy!" Chase snarled. "I told you not to go down into the mine, but away you went and brought the whole goddamn roof down on your head."

Willy's smile wavered but didn't die. "It was an accident, Chase. I sure enough didn't bring it down on me on purpose, and that's a fact."

"You've been nothing but trouble to me since the day you were born," Chase complained, his face contorted with rage. His lips barely moved as he spat out the bitter words.

"You always followed me around like a lost dog. You were always underfoot. Always in my way. You weren't ever worth so much as the powder it would take to blow you up. It seems I just never could get shut of you. Not even this time!"

Willy's smile finally died. "Chase, you sound like you *wished* you could get shut of me. Like you wished I'd died down here under all those rocks. You don't mean that, do you, Chase? Tell me what you really mean so I can get it straight in my mind."

"You got it straight as an arrow."

"No," Willy said after a long moment, shaking his head in disbelief. "No, Chase, you don't mean that. I'm your *brother.*"

"What you are is a millstone around my neck. You've been one since the day you were born. But I thought I was shut of you once and for all when I left you behind in Kansas City that time. I never wanted you with me, but there you were one day sitting on my doorstep after you'd tracked me down, though God only knows how you ever managed to do it."

"I wanted to be with you, Chase," Willy said as if he were explaining the matter as clearly as he could. "After Pa died, there wasn't no point in staying on at home. There was only me after that, so after I buried him I thought I'd come a'hunting you so I'd have somebody to be with. But then you run off on me in Kansas City, like you said. Only I didn't know you'd run off on me at the time. I reckoned you'd just had some more trouble with the law and had to hightail it out of town. So I went looking for you again."

"And may God damn the day you found me again!"

"Chase, I didn't know—I mean you never came right out and said you didn't want me around."

Willy tried another smile. It didn't work. He nodded, his lips quivering as if he were silently talking to himself—or as if he was about to cry.

Chase pulled away from the wall and strode down the tunnel. A moment later he disappeared from sight.

Willy glanced at Barclay. "Chase, he's just upset about what happened to me down here. He gets edgy when things go wrong. That's on account of he's got a nervous nature. Don't take what he says serious, because half the time Chase don't mean a single thing he says."

"Willy, I'm going to piggyback you out of here," Barclay said, thinking that the boy loved his brother so much he wouldn't face the fact that Chase had no more use for him than a flea has for a long-dead dog.

Barclay bent over and Pardue helped Willy climb onto the doctor's back. When the boy's arms were wrapped around Barclay's neck, the doctor followed Pardue down the tunnel and then up the steep slope of the shaft into the last light of the day.

"I'm going to need some wood to splint the boy's leg with," he told Pardue as he eased Willy off his back and down to the ground. "About this long," he said, holding his hands a foot and a half apart. "You think you can find me some?"

"Be back as soon as I can," Pardue said and left.

He was as good as his word. He returned within ten minutes carrying a bundle of limbs he had stripped from a ponderosa pine. "Will these do?" he asked Barclay.

"They'll do fine, Ben. Thank you. If you'd cut off those branches I'd appreciate it. I have to lash the splint tightly to the limb, and the least little bump is going to feel like somebody set Willy's leg on fire."

Barclay use his knife to slit Willy's jeans and then cut them off just above the boy's knee. He tore the cloth into long strips and set them on the ground next to his patient. Then, kneeling next to Willy, he said, 'I'm going to set your leg now, and I'm afraid it's going to hurt."

"You go ahead and do what's got to be done, Doc."

Barclay looked down at Willy's left leg which he had bared, noting the angle at which it canted. He took the limb in both hands above and below the knee and began to straighten it, proceeding slowly in order not to damage the tissue around the site of the break.

Looking up as Willy let out a tortured *"Oh, my!"* he saw the sweat blossoming on the boy's face and the trembling of his lips.

"Ben," he said, "get a bullet for him to bite on."

Pardue went over to where Chase was standing some distance away and spoke to the man. Chase thumbed a cartridge out of his belt and handed it to Pardue, who brought it back and placed it between Willy's teeth.

"I'm almost finished," Barclay said as Willy bit down on the bullet and squeezed his eyes shut. A moment later he finished setting the broken bone. He picked up the four pine limbs and then proceeded to tie them in place against the injured leg, using strips of the cloth that had once been part of Willy's jeans.

"There you go," he said when he had the splints in place. "That leg of yours ought to heal just fine. With a little luck, it'll mend as straight as it ever was."

Willy removed the bullet from between his teeth. "Thanks, Doc," he murmured. Then he fainted.

Willy ate heartily that night, the boiled rice dotted with dried raisins vanishing from his plate in minutes.

"Do you want some more?" Betsy asked Barclay as she stirred the pot that hung suspended from a metal bar over the fire.

"No, thank you. I'm filled up to the ears. It was very good, Betsy."

"Anybody can boil rice and throw in a few raisins," she said modestly, but she was obviously pleased by Barclay's compliment.

Some distance from the fire, Chase stood beside his horse, drinking a cup of coffee. Next to Barclay was Pardue, hunkered down and also sipping coffee, his empty plate on the ground in front of him.

Above them the moon drifted in a sky filled with stars. In the distance a coyote howled and then howled again, the sound a lonely anthem in the otherwise silent night.

"When I saw Chase come out of that mine alone," Betsy said to Barclay, "I wished I had taken one of your guns off his horse while he was gone. I would have shot him with it right between the eyes."

"Why didn't you get yourself a gun?"

"I thought you'd all come out of the mine together and I wouldn't be able to get a clear shot at Chase. I thought I might hit you or Sergeant Pardue."

Betsy rose. "You sure you don't want some more rice and raisins? There's some left."

"I'm sure. I'll have a cup of coffee, though."

As Barclay started to rise, Betsy gestured to indicate he was to stay where he was. She poured a cup of coffee and brought it to him.

Barclay thanked her and watched her circle the fire and begin retrieving their dirty plates. Then he turned his attention to Chase, who was staring into the fire.

That man has meanness in him, Barclay thought. Maybe even madness. It could be seen in the faint sneer that never seemed to leave his face, even when, as now, that face was in relative repose. It could be heard in his voice, which contained a barely disguised contempt for those to whom he spoke.

If I do find the gold, Barclay thought, *Chase will probably kill me. He won't need me anymore and he won't want to share the gold with either me or Pardue. He'll probably kill us both.*

What could he do then to avoid that possibility before it turned into a brutal fact?

As he sat sipping his coffee, Barclay considered several options. He could try to get his hands on one or both of his guns. He could make his move when Chase went to sleep tonight. But what would he do if he got a gun in his hands? Shoot Chase? Kill him? He was sure he couldn't do such a cold-blooded thing, not even to save his own life.

But with Pardue's and maybe even Betsy's help he would be able to get the drop on Chase and tie him up. That idea appealed to him. But he doubted that such a plan would work. Chase was a wary man. Taking him by surprise would be no easy task. It might even prove to be an impossible one.

Still, something had to be done, he knew, or he was sure he was going to die. Perhaps he could lead the party away from the gold. But how long could he practice such procrastination? Surely Chase would lose patience in time.

"Ben," he said, "I've been thinking about what we can do concerning this bad situation we find ourselves in."

"What did you come up with, Captain?"

"We've got to attempt to escape."

Pardue looked at him with a surprised expression on his face. "Escape, Captain? Do you really think that's a good idea?"

"I think it's worth a try."

"Chase would shoot us if he caught us trying to escape."

"I don't think so. He wouldn't want to kill me, because if he did he'd have next to no chance of finding the gold on his own."

"That's true enough. But what about me? Chase has no reason in the world to keep from stopping my clock."

"I've considered that fact. I don't like to say this, Ben, but I think Chase is going to kill the pair of us once the gold is found. And if the gold is not found—well, I think we'll meet with the same fate."

Pardue pondered Barclay's words. Then he said, "I reckon you're right, Captain. It looks like we can't win whichever way the cards fall."

"That, my friend, makes escape a very attractive option."

"You don't think we should stick it out and take our chances with Chase? I mean, maybe he would give us a share of the gold and let us go."

Barclay said, "I'm convinced he'll kill us."

Pardue sighed. "When do we try to hightail it out of here?"

"Tonight when they're all asleep we'll get our guns and horses and be gone."

"I've got an idea, Captain. I'll go on over to Chase and tell him I'll picket our horses for the night. I'll take them away from our camp here. That way, with the horse picketed far enough away from camp, we won't have to worry about anybody hearing us when we light a shuck later tonight."

"Good idea."

Pardue rose and rounded the fire. Seconds later he was engaged in an earnest conversation with Chase.

Chapter Nine

Barclay lay sleepless, his eyes closed, listening to the sounds around him.

Someone was snoring. Someone else was softly whistling as he—or she—breathed noisily. An owl hooted. Something scampered lightly along the ground next to where Barclay lay wrapped in his bedroll.

He turned over, opened his eyes, and saw Willy lying close to the fire, his lips parted and his eyelids flickering. Chase was on the other side of the fire, wrapped in a blanket that hid his face. Betsy was curled up in a ball under a tarp; she was the one who was snoring. Next to him, Pardue lay flat on his back, his face covered by his hat.

"Ben," Barclay whispered.

From beneath the hat came the murmured words, "Time to make our move, Captain?"

"They're all asleep, as far as I can tell."

Pardue sat up and pushed his hat back on his head. "I wish I'd been able to convince Chase to let me move the horses away from the camp. But he wouldn't hear of it. Claimed Apaches might make off with them."

"Do you think we ought to try to get back our weapons?" Barclay asked.

"Too risky. When Chase took them off his horse along with his bedroll, he practically lay down on top of them. No, Captain, we'll have to kiss those guns good-bye. We could never get them without waking him up."

Barclay threw off his blanket. He slowly rose to his feet. He beckoned to Pardue, who got up and began to follow him around the perimeter of the camp where the shadows were thickest and the light of the low-burning fire could not reach them.

When the sole of his boot scraped noisily across a stone, he froze, standing motionless in the moon light, his eyes on the three sleepers in the distance.

None of them moved.

Barclay moved closer to the horses, peering at the ground in front of him to avoid twigs and stones.

When they reached the spot where the horses had been picketed by Chase, Barclay stood close to his mount and gently stroked its nose. He continued doing so while Pardue began to saddle the horse, which nickered once, causing both men to drop down.

No one woke.

Minutes later, Pardue had Barclay's horse saddled. "Hold the bridle chain in your hand to keep it from jingling," he told Barclay in a whisper, once he had the bit in place.

Then, when he had saddled and bridled his own horse, he gestured to Barclay. With his hand gripping his own bridle chain to keep it from jingling, Pardue began to lead his horse away from the campsite.

Barclay followed him, maneuvering around the other saddles, blankets, and bridles, which were piled on the ground near the spot where the horses had been picketed.

"Mount up, Captain. It's time we shook the dust of this place off of us."

As Pardue swung into the saddle, Barclay placed a foot in a stirrup and was about to lift himself up. But, before he could, Chase's voice snarled, "Don't move, either of you, or there'll be two new men stoking the fires of hell tonight."

Barclay turned and saw Chase sitting astride his horse, the other man's long gun aimed directly at him.

"You two almost pulled it off," he said with a mirthless smile. "Almost, but not quite. I'm a light sleeper. I heard you pussy-footing around."

"How come you didn't shoot us?" Pardue asked.

"That's easy enough to answer. If I killed the good doctor, how would I ever find the gold without him to guide me to it? As for you, Sergeant, let's say I didn't shoot you out of the pure goodness of my heart."

"Run for it, Captain!" Pardue suddenly shouted, slamming his heels into his mount's flanks.

Barclay was about to climb aboard his horse when Chase fired, spooking the doctor's horse, which shied, then reared and galloped away, knocking Barclay to the ground in the process.

For an instant Barclay was paralyzed, unable to move and unsure of what to do. Then, recovering his wits, he got to his feet and sprinted off in the direction Pardue had taken.

Chase fired again.

Barclay heard the round whine past his left ear before it slammed into the canyon wall and sent granite dust showering down to the ground.

He ran as fast as he could until he heard sounds up ahead. He saw Pardue galloping back toward him and ran to meet the man, guessing what the sergeant had in mind.

Pardue drew rein and his horse skidded to a halt not far from Barclay. "Climb up, Captain" he yelled and held out his hand.

Barclay ran to take it. But before he could make contact with Pardue and swing up behind him, another shot sounded and Pardue lost control of his frightened horse as it bolted.

"Split up!" he shouted to Barclay as he fought to regain control of his mount. "Weaver's Needle!" he yelled over his shoulder before his horse bore him around a bend in the canyon and out of sight.

Barclay raced in the opposite direction, Pardue's last words echoing in his ear. Weaver's Needle. Pardue must have meant that they should meet later at the tall peak that bore that name. As he sped through the night, Barclay became aware of the sound of hoofbeats coming from somewhere behind him. Chase, no doubt. He ran faster.

He never saw the rotting deadfall that tripped him and sent him sprawling facedown on the ground, because the moon had momentarily vanished in the clouds.

He lay stunned on the ground, his world whirling around him in a dizzy series of shifting arcs. He blinked, trying to bring things into focus. He shook his head in an attempt to clear it. The last maneuver worked reasonably well. Soon he could see clearly again.

He got to his feet and stood swaying slightly as his vision began to blur again. His heart began to thud in his chest as he heard the sound of hoofbeats moving in his direction. Chase or Pardue?

He couldn't wait here to find out. He had to hide. If it turned out to be Chase coming toward him . . .

He began to run, aimlessly at first, past a long ragged row of multiarmed cholla cactus standing like silent sentinels in the desert night.

Behind him the sound of hoofbeats grew louder, and he realized more than one horse was heading in his direction.

He looked back over his shoulder as he ran, but he could see nothing. A moment later he bit down on his lower lip to keep himself from screaming as he stumbled and accidentally brushed against one of the cholla and the plant's spines ripped into the flesh of his left arm through his shirt sleeve.

The moon slid out from behind the clouds and brightened the night.

Barclay, looking around him as he fled, could see no place where he could go to ground. There was absolutely no place for him to hide from whoever was on his back trail. He looked up at the ridge above him, then he turned to the right and headed up the steep slope of the canyon. His breath was coming in short, desperate bursts now, but he kept doggedly on, determined to reach the ridge and drop down beyond it.

He had just crested the ridge and thrown himself down to the ground when two riders came into view below him.

Pardue was in the lead. Chase, his saddle gun cradled in his right arm, rode directly behind the man he had apparently run down and taken prisoner.

Barclay watched them ride on until they were directly below him, at which point Chase called a halt. He sat his horse, scanning the area for Barclay, who remained well hidden on the ridge. Then Chase and Pardue moved on. They rounded a bend in the canyon and disappeared from sight.

Barclay shifted position so that he was sitting just below the rim of the ridge in a kind of cleft in the rocks. The movement caused pain in his left arm, which he proceeded to examine. Cactus burrs were deeply embedded in the flesh, and he knew he had to get them out before they became infected.

He slid his knife from its sheath, which hung from his belt, and, bracing himself, began to dig the sharp spines from his flesh with the sharp point of the blade. He gritted his teeth against the searing pain his efforts were causing him until finally the last of the long-barbed burrs was removed. He leaned back and sighed with relief.

He recalled an old soldier at Fort McDowell telling a chilling tale about an incident he had witnessed during the campaigns against the Apaches in Arizona Territory in the late sixties. The old-timer said that one of the troop had been captured. The Indians had stripped the man and then thrown him against a jumping cholla. The man's body was speared by the spines of the cactus, which were barbed in the manner of fish hooks. The old soldier said his agonized screams were pitiful to hear. The Indians continued to throw him against the plant every time he managed to scramble, screaming, free of it, his body a bloody pincushion of burrs. The tale-teller had said that there was no torture known to man more excruciating than that inflicted by the barbed spines of the jumping cholla.

Now he knew from firsthand experience that the soldier had been a telling a terrible truth.

He sat there using a handkerchief to mop up the rivulets of blood that were running down his arm. He knew he had to help Ben escape from Chase. He was painfully aware that he was but one man—and a weaponless and unhorsed one at that—against an armed and mounted man. And if Willy were to join forces with his brother . . .

Barclay finally decided he would return to Fort McDowell and explain to Colonel Carstair what had happened. The colonel would send troopers to rescue Pardue and take Chase and his brother into custody. It was, Barclay decided, the only sensible and practical thing he could do under the circumstances.

He rose and began to walk along the ridge, careful to keep away from its rim in order not to outline himself against the sky.

He thought of Eva as he walked. It seemed ages since he had last seen his wife. He visualized her face. He recalled the warmth of her body against his in the days when their love had been as strong as life itself. He suddenly found himself wanting her more than he had ever wanted the gold that lay hidden in the Superstitions. Maybe, once he reached the fort, he would be able to find a way to get her to change her mind and not leave for Boston as she had planned. Maybe he could persuade her to stay with him, and together they would find a way to bring love and happiness back into their lives.

"Barclay!"

He stopped at the sound of Chase shouting his name. He dropped down and then eased himself up along the ridge until he could look over its edge. Below him were Chase and Pardue, Chase holding a revolver on Pardue. Pardue was trailing Barclay's horse, which he or Chase had recaptured.

"Come back, Barclay!" Chase shouted as he moved slowly along beside Pardue. "If you do, all will be forgiven! If you don't, your friend Pardue will die. I'll kill him when the sun sets tomorrow!"

As Barclay watched, the loud words causing his skin to crawl, Chase jabbed Pardue in the ribs with the barrel of his gun, and Barclay could see Chase's lips moving.

Then Pardue cupped his hands around his mouth and called out, "Captain, the man means what he says. He'll do me in if you don't come back and show him where the gold is."

Another vicious jab in the ribs from Chase's gun barrel silenced Pardue.

"You've got till sundown tomorrow, Barclay," Chase bellowed. "If you're not back by then—" Chase squeezed a shot into the air.

Pardue flinched. Chase smiled his saturnine smile. Then the pair rode off.

Barclay lay on the ridge, his body tense, his mind in chaos. He knew it was not possible for him to make it to Fort McDowell and back here by sundown tomorrow. If he wanted Pardue to live, he would have to go back to the campsite and continue to hunt for the gold as Chase had just demanded.

"Barclay!"

Chase's voice came to him from a great distance. He could no longer see either Chase or Pardue. He listened to his name echo through the canyon.

"—clay,—clay,—clay."

Then Chase repeated his earlier message, until the echoing words faded away.

Barclay lowered his head, letting his forehead rest on the ground. He took a deep breath. He knew he was beaten. He couldn't let Chase kill Ben.

He got to his feet and started walking along the ridge, heading back toward the campsite in order to save the life of the man who had once saved his when he was attacked by the two would-be robbers in Fort McDowell.

Sadness settled heavily on him as he realized he would now have no opportunity to talk to Eva before she left for Boston.

Now there was no way to stop her from leaving him. He cursed himself for not having stayed at the fort and tried to reason with her. He should have swallowed his pride and his anger and attempted to work something out with her. But, no, both his pride and his anger had stuck in his craw and he simply could not swallow them. Instead he had stormed out of the house like some impetuous fool who was unaware of the loss his action would cause him.

He halted. He didn't have to go back to the campsite. He could turn around and go back to the fort and leave Ben to fend for himself as best he could.

No. He had to reject the idea, much as he wanted to embrace it. He could not abandon Ben. So he would have to suffer the loss of the woman he now knew he loved more than all the gold in the world.

Squaring his shoulders, he walked on.

Dawn was gilding the low line of clouds that ranged just above the horizon when he realized that he had lost his way. He looked around him, wishing he had paid more attention to his surroundings instead of to his tormented thoughts.

Nothing looked familiar. He seemed to have climbed higher into the mountains without being aware of having done so. Looking down, he saw several small valleys that looked like a giant's footprints in the chaparral-covered landscape. Far below him grew mesquite and saguaro cactus while around him were juniper and piñon pine. The desert had gradually given way to grassland.

A sense of urgency seized him as the sun slowly rose above the horizon line to hang blood-red in the blindingly blue sky. When that sun set . . .

He had to find his way back to the campsite, and find it fast. He forced himself to think calmly about the way he had been traveling. He had been on the ridge above the canyon and he had started walking—was it west? Yes, he decided. And the canyon that led to the campsite ran in a west-to-east direction. So he had to turn and retrace his steps.

He hurried back, searching for signs of something familiar. When he found none, his distress grew. He was running when he found himself in a thicket of manzanita bushes, the branches of which tore at him and opened several of his cactus-burr wounds.

The ominous growl that came from somewhere in the rabbit-brush beyond the thicket caused him to swiftly slow his pace. When the growl came again, louder this time, he halted and looked around nervously.

He could see nothing. He wasn't sure exactly where the growl had come from, and he was afraid that he might inadvertently move toward the animal. Finally, knowing he could not stay where he was indefinitely, he took a tentative step to the right.

The puma materialized not five feet in front of him. It seemed to rise out of the ground like a frightening apparition, all steely sinew and thick muscle.

At that moment, the wind shifted. The grasses that had been bending in an easterly direction now leaned to the west. To Barclay the wind brought the smell of dead meat. The puma, he guessed, had made a kill and been feeding on it when he inadvertently intruded upon it. The kill must be lying in the grass where he could not see it.

As the puma bared its teeth and growled again, Barclay took a step backward. At the same time he removed his knife from its sheath. Holding it in his right hand, he took another step backward, resisting the strong impulse to turn and run for his life. He was sure that if he did the puma would come bounding after him.

The wind shifted again. This time it blew toward the puma, carrying to the creature, Barclay realized with horror, the scent of his own blood.

The puma's nostrils quivered. The grasses behind it whipped back and forth as the animal began to nervously twitch its long tail.

It'll go for my neck, Barclay thought.

He continued backing away.

The puma's large golden eyes gleamed, never leaving Barclay.

It took a step forward, its muscles moving beneath its tawny coat. Then it took another step.

It kept its body close to the ground, its belly almost touching the earth as it crept forward, its white teeth bared and glistening, the faint sound of a snarl coming from between its parted lips.

Barclay held his knife with the blade slanted upward. He stopped backing away, forcing himself to make a stand.

A moment later, it did. The puma pounced, gliding gracefully through the air, its front paws outstretched, all its claws spread.

Barclay nimbly stepped to the left. As he did so, the puma sailed past him. He swept the knife upward, intending to gut the animal if he could, but his blade missed its intended target and slashed the animal's shoulder.

The cut was deep enough to cause the puma to scream as it hit the ground nearly two feet behind Barclay. The sound shrilled in the still air, a ghostly kind of keening.

Then the puma turned and sprang again.

Because Barclay had been unprepared for the second attack, the puma's body struck him, knocking him to the ground. He felt the outstretched claws of the animal rake his right forearm. This time it was his turn to scream.

At the same time, he plunged his knife into the body of the puma as it straddled him. He had aimed for the animal's neck, but again he missed his intended target, instead striking the puma's chest.

Blood spurted from the wound Barclay had just inflicted, drenching his face and blinding him. He struggled against his attacker, trying desperately to get out from under the animal. He succeeded in doing so after bringing up one knee and using it to strike a blow that caught the cat in the ribs and knocked it to one side. Scrambling quickly to his feet, Barclay wiped the blood that was blinding him from his eyes and lunged at the puma. It slunk away from him, moving sideways, still snarling deep in its throat, its ears laid sleekly back against its skull.

Now Barclay was the stalker. He followed the cat, moving slowly, never taking his eyes from the animal. This time he

108

had to kill it, because, if he allowed it to attack again, he might not survive. This time, he told himself, his teeth grinding together, is the third time and they say the third time's the charm.

Before he could strike, the puma sprang at him. He swung the knife, cut the cat's leg, swung again, and missed. He backed away, his knife dripping blood on the rabbitbrush underfoot, and stumbled over the puma's prey, the body of a mule deer.

He fell to the ground beside it, dropping his knife as he did so. He caught a glimpse of the deer's viscera lying half-eaten on the ground by his elbow, and then he leaped to his feet as the puma came racing toward him.

When it sprang this time, a shot sounded and the cat, hit in mid-air, convulsed so that its four paws slashed downward, its front paws almost touching those in the rear. Then the animal fell to the ground and lay jerking spasmodically, its eyes beginning to glaze.

Barclay turned and saw the mounted man with the rifle about forty yards from him. The man was grinning, his teeth shining in the sunlight, their white brightness contrasting sharply with the swarthiness of his skin.

Barclay looked down at the dead puma and then, forgetting to retrieve his knife, walked over to where the man was sitting his horse. "I'm tremendously obliged to you," he said and held out his hand.

The man slid out of the saddle and shook hands with Barclay.

He was a tall man with a bent nose and thick lips. Between his nose and lips grew a bushy black mustache whose ends drooped down below his chin. The hair visible under his sombrero was also black.

He wore a dirty white shirt beneath a suede vest and worn trousers tucked into scarred black boots.

"I thank you very much for saving my life," Barclay told him.

"My name, señor, is Angel Torres, and my country is Old Mexico."

"Ralph Barclay. I'm posted at Fort McDowell."

"Fort McDowell is north of here."

The statement sounded like a question. "I'm here in the Superstitions on a scouting mission of sorts."

"Ah, then we are two of a kind, señor. I, too, am here in these mountains on a scouting mission. I hunt for Apaches."

"You hunt Apaches?"

"*Sí*. In my country, the government, she pays money for Apache scalps. Those Indians, they are very much—how you say—the nuisance in my country. They come across the Rio Bravo, steal horses, steal children to make slaves. So I come north to hunt Apaches. It is a very funny thing."

"A funny thing? I'm afraid I don't understand."

"It is this way, señor. In my body is some Apache blood. My mother, she was of the Tonto Apache tribe. So it is a funny thing that I hunt those of my own blood. But a living must be earned, is it not so, señor?"

"You've chosen rather dangerous work, I must say."

Torres shrugged. "Is so. The work it is dangerous. But I have done well. Maybe it is my Apache blood, *sí*? Maybe the Apache part of me keeps the rest of me alive. You have, in your country, señor, a saying. It takes a thief to catch a thief. It takes a part-Apache like me to catch Apache."

"Are there many Apaches in the Superstitions?"

"Plenty Apaches here, *sí*. They are everywhere in the mountains. See that rock?" Torres giggled. "Turn it over, you maybe find Apache under it." He giggled again. "Come. I show you Apache."

"I really don't want to see any Apaches," Barclay said. "I don't want any trouble."

"Ah, señor, you are like horse who sees snake—all shaky inside and out. I make promise to you. This Apache, he do you no harm. This Apache do no more harm to nobody. Me, the Angel of Death, has seen to that."

"You call yourself that—the Angel of Death?"

"Apaches call me that first because of how I kill them. Now I call myself that, too. Nice name, *sí*? Angel of Death?"

Torres beckoned, and Barclay reluctantly followed him up a slope.

Torres pointed to the body of a dead Apache lying next to the ashes of a dying campfire. "I catch him, that one, last night just before sun gone. I shoot him, take his hair. Come, I show you." Torres led the way back to his horse, where he opened his saddlebag and displayed its contents.

Barclay stared in morbid fascination at the scalps the saddlebag contained, many of them obviously fresh, others encrusted with black blood. He looked up at the self-proclaimed Angel of Death, who gave him a proud smile. "Torres, I wonder if you could help me."

"You have 'nother puma for me to shoot?"

Barclay shook his head.

Torres giggled. "What help you need, Ralph Barclay?"

"I'm afraid I'm lost. I was with some people here in the mountains. We made camp yesterday at an abandoned silver mine. I left the camp somewhere, and now I can't find it. Do you know where that silver mine is located?"

"Yes, for sure, I know. Many times Torres spend rainy nights in that mine."

"Could you show me the way to it?"

Torres frowned. "You have no horse?"

"I'm afraid he ran off on me."

"That is too bad. Silver mine is long walk from this place. Why you want to go there? Is no more silver in mine. Is, as you gringos say, 'pinched out' long time ago."

"It isn't the silver I want. I know there's none there. I just want to rejoin the people I was with. I must do so before sunset today, so I would very much appreciate it if you would show me—"

"You go down there," Torres said, pointing past the dead puma. "See there—that pile of rocks?"

Torres glanced at Barclay, who nodded. He then said, "Turn left there. Keep walking. Keep sun behind you. When you see dead saguaro cactus, look at it. See which way its left arm points. Go that way. You will come to canyon. Go down into canyon, turn left, and follow it. You will come to mine pretty soon."

"Again, my thanks, Torres. I wish you luck with your hunting."

"The Angel of Death, he wishes you luck with your hunting. What is it you hunt here in this bad place?"

Barclay hesitated and then decided there was no harm in telling the truth. "Gold."

"Ah, gold. I told you we were two of a kind. You hunt for gold and so do I. Only difference is you hunt for raw gold. I hunt for Apache scalps I can trade in my country for gold."

"My group hasn't found any yet," Barclay volunteered.

"Indians say much gold hidden here in mountains. I pray sometimes for God to show Torres the way to the gold. But He is afraid to do that, I think. He is afraid the Apache thunder gods will become angry with Him if he tells where is their gold.

"But maybe one day I have luck and find the gold. Be rich man in Old Mexico then. Grow fat. Have many women. Much tequila. It is a dream I like to dream."

"It is a dream many men like to dream," Barclay said.

"*Adiós*, Ralph Barclay," Torres said with a wave of his hand. *"Vaya con Dios,"* he added before climbing back into the saddle and riding away.

Chapter Ten

Barclay made his way past the dead bodies of the puma and mule deer and headed for the pile of rocks which lay some distance away at the base of a sharply rising ridge. When he reached them, he turned left as he had been instructed and continued walking.

Later, when he found that the sun was on his right, he remembered Torres's directions and realized he had strayed from the path he should be following. Torres had said to keep the sun behind him as he walked, so Barclay altered his course.

He walked on, setting a steady pace for himself while keeping a sharp lookout for the dead saguaro cactus Torres had told him to look for.

He looked up when he heard sounds above him and saw a herd of bighorns marching along the ridge. He lowered his head as several pebbles that had been dislodged by the sheep came tumbling harmlessly down around him. When he raised his head again, there it was. The dead saguaro was up ahead and a little to the left. He hurried toward it across a wide expanse of lava rock but then halted when he came upon a half-hidden waterhole.

His thirst had been building for some time and seemed to grow stronger as he stared down at the still water. He was repelled by the green film of algae that covered its surface.

His thirst overpowered his repugnance. Kneeling, he told himself that however unappetizing the water might appear, it did support life and that meant that it was not alkaline and probably safe to drink. He brushed away the green surface scum and then scooped up some water in his cupped hands and drank it. He drank again and again, blissfully convinced that he had never tasted sweeter water in his entire life.

Refreshed, his mouth and throat no longer parched, he was about to rise and resume his journey when he heard a sharp cracking sound from far above him. He looked up and was horrified to see a portion of the ridge above him give way and break into pieces under the stress of the passing bighorns. As the rocky missiles came careening down toward him, he sprang to his feet and ran, but he was too late. A slab of rock struck him on the head, knocking him to the ground.

He fought to remain conscious, but he quickly lost the fight as he slipped into total darkness.

When he regained consciousness, the sun was making a slow descent toward the western horizon.

He groaned and sat up. He raised a hand and gingerly touched the throbbing spot on his forehead where the slab of rock had struck him. He felt the crust of blood that covered most of his right temple. Then he got shakily to his feet. Steadying himself as best he could, he headed toward the saguaro cactus in the distance. When he reached it, he recalled Torres's words. *When you see dead saguaro cactus, look at it. See which way its right arm points. Go that way. You will come to canyon.*

The right arm of the cactus pointed to the northwest so Barclay headed northwest, his anxiety growing with every step he took as he continued trying to reach his destination before the sun set and Chase Ransom murdered Ben Pardue.

Twenty minutes later he still had not come to the canyon that

Torres had told him he would reach, the one through which he could pass to find the silver mine. He was traveling over gently rolling land sprinkled with barrel cactus and chaparral. He could not remember having seen any barrel cactus since coming into the mountains. Off to his right were twin peaks, one slightly smaller than the other, both of them totally barren. He could not recall having seen them before, either.

He hurried on as the sun slowly sank toward the horizon. Had he come the wrong way? Had he made a wrong turn somewhere? Why did everything look so unfamiliar?

He stepped over a pinacate beetle he had disturbed and which, in a defensive move, had raised its abdomen and secreted a foul-smelling substance.

As the frothy clouds drifting in the sky above him gradually turned golden as the sun sank lower in the western sky, a dispirited Barclay came to a halt. He stood looking around, searching for the reassuring sight of some familiar terrain.

In his mind, he went back over the instructions Torres had given him. He was to go down to the pile of rocks and turn left there. Then he was to walk keeping the sun behind him. When he came to the dead saguaro cactus the Angel of Death had mentioned, he was to note in what direction the plant's right arm pointed. . . .

Something was wrong. Barclay could sense it, but he could not identify what it was that was wrong. He went over Torres's instructions again, reliving in his mind the journey he had just taken. The rocks where he had turned left . . .

Suddenly he had it.

When he came to the cactus, Torres had told him to travel in the direction that the plant's *left*, not right, arm pointed!

Furious with himself for having made a mistake that had cost him so much precious time, he turned and ran back the way he had come—past the twin peaks that loomed in the distance and through the stand of ocotillo bushes. Finally, breathless and sweating profusely, he once again reached the dead saguaro.

This time, after noting the direction in which the saguaro's left arm was pointing, he ran in a southeasterly direction.

He could no longer see the sun. It was hidden now by a volcanic mountain range. From behind the protruding cones of the range, the sun's rays still brightened the sky, turning it from a bright blue to a pale gold.

Up ahead of him, a roadrunner cut across his path. When he nearly caught up with it, it ran faster, its wings flapping in fright as if Barclay were pursuing it.

With the deadline Chase had set for him firmly in mind, he continued his journey, and it was with an overpowering sense of relief that he finally arrived at the ridge above the canyon that he knew would take him to the campsite. He started down the sloping canyon wall. Within seconds, the pace of his descent quickened involuntarily and he lost his balance and rolled down into the canyon's deep chasm.

He picked himself up and, ignoring his bruises and torn clothes, ran on through the thick purple shadows that filled the canyon. Above him the yellow sky was a broad band of light.

He was close to exhaustion when he finally arrived at the campsite and dropped down on the ground near the ashes of the previous night's fire. He sat there, his knees raised, his forearms resting on them, and his head resting on his forearms.

"Well, well, well," he heard Chase say. "The prodigal returns. Would that we had a fatted calf ready for the slaughter so we could celebrate this most auspicious event."

"You had yourself a fatted calf ripe for the slaughter," Barclay heard an angry Pardue snarl. "Me."

"You all right, Captain?" the sergeant asked a moment later, as he dropped down on one knee beside Barclay and gripped the doctor's shoulder. "You look like you've been to Hades and back."

"I'm all right, Ben, thanks. I did have a rather rough go."

"I told you he'd hear me," Pardue said to no one in particular. "I told you he'd rejoin us to save the life of his good friend, Sergeant Pardue."

Betsy came over and knelt next to Barclay. She took his hand in hers and said, "I'm glad you came back, Doc."

"Now we can get on with it," Chase crowed.

"You plan on hunting gold in the middle of the night?" Pardue bellowed incredulously.

"No, of course not," Chase responded easily. "But tomorrow at first light, off we go."

"Where's Willy?" Barclay asked, looking around and seeing no sign of Chase's brother.

"Gone," Pardue answered.

Before the sergeant could say anything else, Chase said, "Betsy, stir yourself and get some wood for a fire. I'm hungry, woman, so *move!*"

Betsy patted Barclay's hand, glared at Chase, and got up in search of wood.

"That's a pretty nasty wound you've got there, Captain," Pardue said, pointing to Barclay's head.

"An accident."

"I have to say I'm glad you came back before the sun went down. If you hadn't Chase would have done me in for sure out of plain cussedness. The man's as mean as a stepped-on sidewinder, Captain."

"What would he have to gain by killing you?"

"Nothing. But consider the matter the other way around. What would he have to lose?"

"I see your point."

"A man that would want to leave one of his own blood to die down in a mine shaft—a man like that is capable of just about anything."

"I'm sure you're right."

"He figured he had nothing to lose by yelling that he was fixing to do me in. The way it worked out, he won. You heard him and you're here to hunt for the gold for him. I reckon I won, too, but maybe you shouldn't have come back, Captain. Now we're both in hot water up to our ears again."

"I had to come back, Ben. I couldn't do otherwise under the circumstances."

"I'm obliged to you, Captain, I truly am."

"Was it you who found my horse?"

"The very same. I'd meant to trail him along while I went to meet you at Weaver's Needle. Then I'd figured on both of us getting ourselves out of these mountains. But Chase cut me off and got the drop on me. He's a sneaky son of a bitch, Captain. He come up on me as slick as shit on a stick, he did. Before I even knew he was anywhere about, there he was, grinning that grin of his and aiming his gun at my gizzard. He had me dead to rights."

"What did he do with our guns?"

"He's got them stashed away over there with his bedroll and tarp. He keeps an eagle eye on them, too, I can tell you."

"I see the mules' loads have been unpacked."

"Chase and Willy did that before Willy left. Chase decided this spot was going to be our base of operations."

"Where is Willy, by the way?"

Pardue picked up a twig and traced a design on the ground.

"Ben, did you hear me?"

"Willy's gone. He's been gone since right after Chase caught me."

"Gone? Where?"

"I wish you hadn't asked me that."

"Why, Ben? What's wrong? What's bothering you?"

"It's your missus, that's what."

"Eva? What do you mean?"

Pardue snapped the twig in two and threw the pieces away. "What happened was, we came back here, Chase and me, after he caught me, and he stormed about the camp something fierce, saying he'd let you get away and he couldn't be sure you'd heard him howling out there in the wilderness for you to come on back to camp and if you didn't come back he was never going to see a nugget of that gold that's up here in the mountains somewheres. He sure did take on for a spell."

"Ben, please. What has all this got to do with Eva?"

"It started out with Betsy. She went to Chase and settled him down some. Then she told him about the night you spent with her back in Phoenix. She told him how you told her that you had told your missus about how you'd memorized as much as you could about the terrain you went over with that Injun. She said you told the missus all about what you saw once the blindfold was taken off at the spot where the gold was."

Understanding suddenly came to Barclay. "Willy's gone to bring Eva here!"

Pardue hung his head. "I'm afraid that's so, Captain. Like I said, it was Betsy's idea. She told Chase if you didn't come back, he could shoot me dead and then they'd wait till Willy got here with Mrs. Barclay and then she could lead them to where the gold is at. She said they didn't need you. Not if they had your missus to take your place, they didn't. So Chase sent Willy to get your lady. Captain, I told you you never should have got mixed up with that whore. If you hadn't, none of this would be happening now. I know I got no right to criticize—"

"You have every right, Ben. You also have every right to name me the damned fool I obviously have been. My God, if Willy does trick Eva into coming here with him, what will happen to her with a man as ruthless as Chase around?"

Pardue had no answer to Barclay's question.

"Damn that Betsy Whitcomb!" Barclay muttered, slamming a fist down on the ground. He sprang to his feet and hurried over to where Betsy was fanning the flames of the fire.

"Why, Betsy?" he asked her, his voice strained. "Why did you do it?"

"Why did I do what?"

"Tell them what I told Eva."

"You really don't know why? I'm surprised at you, Doc. I told you that the gold means a chance for a new life to me. And when Chase brought Pardue back here and said he'd lost your trail, I saw my chance falling to pieces right before my eyes. But then I remembered what you told me about you wife and what you told her about going after the gold. I decided to tell Chase."

"Damn you, Betsy Whitcomb! Damn you to hell!"

Betsy chuckled at Barclay's anger, which suffused his face with a crimson blush. Hands planted on her hips, she threw back her head and laughed into the deepening darkness.

Barclay struck her with the flat of his hand, leaving a red mark on her left cheek.

She responded by attacking him. Pummeling him with her fists, she cursed him, called him "a lily-livered sawbones without either balls or brains."

He gripped her wrists and held her away from him as she tossed her head from side to side in impotent fury. When her rage finally subsided, he released her and pushed her away from him.

Shaking a finger at her, he said, "I'll never forgive you for what you've done. And if Eva is indeed brought here and anything happens to her, I shall see to it that you suffer for it."

Betsy spat on him before turning and stalking away to where an amused Chase had been watching the heated exchange.

They rode out of camp before dawn the next morning with Barclay in the lead, Pardue riding beside him, and Chase and Betsy behind them.

False dawn was beginning to brighten the sky, and on the mesa above them a meadowlark sang as Barclay led the way north through the canyon. He remembered that while blindfolded he had traveled for what seemed to be nearly two hours through a gorge—perhaps this very canyon.

But it might not have been this canyon, he knew, because its entrance had not looked exactly like the entrance to the canyon he had entered after Chunz had blindfolded him. For one thing, there had been no sign of a stream at the entrance to this canyon.

Later, after the sun had risen and they emerged from the canyon, Barclay had to admit to Chase that he had the wrong trail. "I saw no north–south-running canyon along the way," he said, "and the Indian and I stopped at one. That was where Chunz removed my blindfold. We'll have to go back to the lowlands and explore some other canyon leading into the mountains."

"What if that one proves to be the wrong one, like this one did?" a surly Chase wanted to know.

"We keep at it," Barclay said with more optimism than he was feeling. "One of those canyons that begins back on the plain has to be the one I rode into the first time I came here."

They turned their horses and headed back the way they had come.

By the time they rode out of the mountains, the sun was high in the sky. Barclay rode in a northeasterly direction as he searched for the mouth of a canyon that had a growth of scrub pine and ocotillo around it, a creek that formed a tiny waterfall nearby, and a view of four jagged peaks in the distance.

He found none that precisely fitted the place he remembered. He finally chose a canyon from which the four peaks could be seen but which had no creek near it and only a single ocotillo bush beside its mouth.

He led the way into the canyon he had chosen, which was wider than the previous one they had explored. As they rode through a thick patch of chaparral, they flushed a pair of civet cats from cover. The animals went bounding away, their black and white tails bouncing behind them.

They spent the rest of the day traveling throughout the area. They were tired and hungry when they finally returned to camp after sunset.

They had finished their supper when Chase got up and came over to where Barclay was sitting some distance away from the fire.

As the doctor looked up, Chase said, "It's crossed my mind again that maybe you don't want to find the gold that's up here."

Barclay said nothing.

"Could that be the case, Doctor?" Chase asked, nudging Barclay's leg with the toe of his boot.

"It is not the case."

"You're sure about that, are you?"

"I'm sure."

"That's good, because if you were stalling—well, I wouldn't like that one little bit. To make sure you're not stalling, I've got a proposition—no, an ultimatum—to present to you, Doctor. I'm giving you two more days to find the gold. If you haven't found it by sundown of the day after tomorrow, I'll shoot you and your friend here."

"You're one crazy son of a bitch!" Pardue interjected. "If you shoot the captain, you'll never get your hands on the gold."

"I know that," Chase said evenly. "But, like I just told you boys, in two days, if no gold has been found, I'm moving on."

He looked down at Barclay. "I hope you're not stalling, Doctor. If you are, you've got two days to quit playing that game and lead us all to where we want to go. If you keep playing your little game—"

"I've not been stalling. I've just not been able to locate the vein."

"—you're going to die. Now wouldn't it be a shame if Willy does bring your wife up here and all she gets for her trouble is her husband's cold corpse?"

When Chase had gone, Pardue muttered an oath under his breath.

"He's got me in a neat little trap," Barclay said softly. "I'd had it in mind to come back here so he wouldn't shoot you and then, first chance we got, I thought we could get away again.

"But then I ran into the fact that Chase sent Willy to bring Eva here. How can I think of escaping when she may be on her way here right now? Meanwhile—"

"You've got to search for the gold."

"That's right."

"Captain, I hope you won't get mad at me, but I'd like to ask you something."

"What is it?"

"*Have* you been stalling? Have you been leading Chase on a wild-goose chase?"

"No, I haven't. I told him the truth. I've just not been able to find it. All the natural features look too much alike. But I will tell you this, Ben. The thought did cross my mind."

By midafternoon of the following day, Barclay had still not

found the location of the gold although he, together with Pardue and Chase, had been looking since first light.

They were following a zigzag trail through a rugged area full of jagged rocks when the first of the thick thunderheads swept in over a crest ahead of them. The clouds seemed to hang just above the crest, churning and darkening.

"We're going to get wet, Captain," Pardue predicted.

Minutes later the sky burst above them and torrents of rain pelted down. Lightning blazed in the sky, leaping from cloud to black cloud.

Barclay pulled the collar of his shirt up around his neck, a useless gesture, since the rain soon soaked them all to the skin.

Thunder rumbled and roared through the mountains around them.

"The thunder gods," Pardue remarked. "They've finally found us out."

Barclay shivered as the cold rain chilled him to the bone.

"This is a waste of a man's good time," Chase grumbled from behind them. "If you don't find the goddamn gold, and find it soon, it's going to give me one world of pleasure to put a bullet in your brain."

Barclay shivered again but not because he was cold.

Pardue lowered his head, and the rain ran from his hat onto the neck of his horse.

"Watch for a place to get out of this downpour," Barclay told him.

Although they scouted for shelter as they rode on, they found none.

The rain ended fifteen minutes after it had begun. The lightning lessened. The thunder muttered now instead of roaring or rumbling, and then the clouds began to break up. Half an hour later, the sky was clear and the sun was shining again.

"What do you say we call it a day, Chase?" Barclay called over his shoulder.

"No," came Chase's answer. "We keep on."

They kept on.

"Hold it, Captain," Pardue said, holding up a hand at the sound of a howl.

"That sounded like a person crying out," Barclay said, drawing rein.

"It did," Pardue agreed. "At least, it didn't sound like any animal I ever heard before. It came from beyond that butte up there."

Barclay glanced over his shoulder at Chase, who had also halted and was sitting with his hands draped around his saddle horn, listening intently.

The howling came again, louder this time and much more intense.

That's the sound of someone in pain, Barclay thought. "We'd better turn back, Chase," he advised. "There's no telling what might lie up ahead of us."

"Maybe those thunder gods you told Betsy about have caught somebody trying to steal their gold," Chase commented. "Let's have a look."

"It could be Apaches," Pardue warned.

Chase responded by drawing his revolver and ordering Pardue and Barclay to move on.

They moved out, heading for the butte. When they reached it, they dismounted, and, still under Chase's gun, Barclay and Pardue scrambled up the butte's sloping side until they came to a mesa at its summit. There they dropped down, flattening themselves on the hard, grassless ground. Chase took up a similar position to their right.

All three men stared down at the spectacle unfolding below them.

Four Apaches, their half-naked bodies wet with rain, their leggings also wet and sagging soggily around their legs, were standing, sitting, or kneeling about a white man they had stripped naked and staked spread-eagled on the ground.

Barclay felt a chill of fear as he recognized the Apaches. They were the four he had seen when he had been traveling to the Superstitions with Chunz—Eskiminzin and his men. He recalled

Chunz's warning. The man had said Eskiminzin and his braves would kill any white man they found trying to take away their thunder gods' gold.

Barclay's eyes narrowed. "Good Lord!" he exclaimed. "I know that man those savages have staked down!"

"You know him?" Pardue asked. "Who is he?"

"His name is Angel Torres. He calls himself the Angel of Death. I met him after you and I split up following our escape. He's here in the mountains collecting Apache scalps. He told me the Mexican government is paying a bounty on them."

Barclay stared in horror at Torres, who, he was now able to see, had been staked down on a bed of cactus that had been prepared for him by the Indians. Every time he made a move within the tight constraints of the rawhide thongs, he screamed as thorns and burrs bit into his body.

"What's wrong with his right hand?" Pardue asked and then answered his own question. "It's burned, that's what's wrong with it. Those red-skinned devils built a fire in the palm of his hand. The rain put it out. Christ on the cross, you can see the bones in his hand!"

Barclay watched, horrified, as one of the Apaches kindled a fire on the ashes of one that had gone out. When it was blazing, he removed a burning brand from it with the aid of two sticks and then dropped it in Torres's left palm.

Torres howled, his head thrashing from side to side, blood dripping from the lips he had bitten through in his pain-maddened frenzy.

The brand burned for a long time before it finally went out.

The Apache who had placed it in Torres's palm laughed along with his companions and then methodically proceeded to heap burning brands on Torres's groin.

"What did he say?" Barclay asked Pardue as Torres screamed a string of words in Spanish.

"I didn't understand every word, Captain. I told you my Mex is not that good. But best as I could tell, he called on the mother of God to put him out of his misery."

Barclay, not a religious man, nevertheless found himself silently praying a similar prayer.

More frantic words flew from Torres's bloody lips.

"He's begging those savages to kill him," Pardue said in a tense tone. "Let's get out of here, Captain. I've not got the stomach for this."

As Pardue began to scramble crabwise back along the mesa, Chase said, "Stay put, soldier."

Pardue froze as Chase took aim at him.

"I want to see how this winds up," Chase said. "Get back up there."

Pardue reluctantly obeyed the order, but when he was once again beside Barclay, he kept his eyes closed as Torres's screams rose and fell and finally stopped altogether after a long and terrible time.

Barclay, sickened, stared down at the charred flesh of Torres's hands and at the gaping hole where his genitals had been and where now partially charred bones were visible. Barclay was barely aware of the four Apaches who were mounting their ponies and riding off, leaving their lifeless victim behind them.

"They'll be rounding the butte in a matter of minutes," he heard himself say dully to Chase. "If we don't get out of here, we're going to die the same way Torres did."

"So what are we waiting for?" Chase asked rhetorically. "Let's go. The showdown below's all over. But it was fun while it lasted, wasn't it, gents?"

Chapter Eleven

There was white, red, and black paint on the faces of the Indians. In their hands were lances.

Barclay was weaponless and had no choice but to run from them. Through a landscape of sharp rocks he ran. Moonlight was denied him by black clouds in a blacker sky. His ears recorded the heart-stopping cries of the pursuing savages.

He didn't dare look back over his shoulder. He was afraid of what he would see. He wondered where Eva was. He thanked God that she was not here with him. The Indians would— He didn't dare continue the thought.

He climbed a mountain. He swam a river. So did the Indians, relentless in their pursuit of him.

When the arrows began to fly around him, he ran faster, as fast as he possibly could. With the speed of a zebra he ran. When an arrow struck him and buried its sharp stone head in his back, he screamed.

"Easy, Captain! Wake up now. Come on, Captain, wake up."

Barclay's eyes snapped open. He pushed himself up on his

elbows. Odd that the moon was visible in the sky now. All around him was silence except for the soothing sound of Pardue's voice.

"You must have had a nightmare, Captain. You let out a yell in your sleep that was loud enough to wake the dead."

A nightmare. Yes, that's what it was. Not a dream. A nightmare.

"I was dreaming of Apaches, Ben," Barclay said as he sat up and looked around. "They were after me. They were trying to kill me."

Pardue coughed and then cleared his throat. "Speaking of killing, Captain, today's the day."

For a moment Barclay didn't know what Pardue was talking about. But then it came to him. Today was the deadline Chase had given him. At sunset tonight, Chase said he intended to kill both him and Pardue if he had not found the gold by then.

"Are you feeling lucky, Captain?" Pardue asked him with a wary smile. "I hope so. This is our last chance."

"Willy's not back?"

"Nope."

Willy should have been back by now, Barclay thought. Hope flooded his heart. Maybe Willy had not been able to persuade Eva to come to the campsite with him. Or maybe she'd already left the fort. Barclay prayed that was the case.

His prayer was interrupted when he heard a muffled voice call out from the darkness beyond the low-burning campfire, "Hello, the camp!"

Barclay strained to catch a glimpse of the visitor, but he could see nothing.

Chase sat up, throwing off his blanket and going for his gun. "Who's out there?" he shouted.

"Howdy, Chase," Willy said as he rode out of the shadows and into the camp.

Barclay's heart leaped at the sight of Eva seated behind Willy. Then his heart sank as he thought that now she, too, was a prisoner of Chase Ransom.

"Ralph!" Eva cried when she caught sight of him. "Ralph, are you all right?"

Barclay rose and went over to her as Willy, with the help of a tree limb he had padded and was using as a crutch, got out of the saddle. He helped Eva down from Willy's horse and took her into his arms. "I'm all right, Eva."

"Oh, I'm so glad!" Eva hugged Barclay tightly, her cheek pressed against his chest. Then, drawing back, she said, "But you've been hurt. Your temple. Your arm. What happened to you?"

Barclay told her about his cactus injury and about having been struck by a falling rock.

"Who are these people?" Eva asked when he had finished. "Why was I brought here?"

"Because of the gold," Barclay told her. "I made the mistake of telling the woman over there that I was setting out to hunt for gold. She asked to come along, and I agreed to take her. Her gentleman friend—that man over there is Chase Ransom—found out about our search and invited himself and his brother, Willy, along."

"Have you found the gold?"

"No, we haven't. That's why Chase sent Willy to bring you here, Eva."

"I'm afraid I don't understand."

Barclay explained.

After he had finished, Eva looked at him incredulously. "Chase Ransom thinks *I* can lead him to the gold?"

"That's right, Mrs. Barclay," Chase said, holstering his gun and strolling over to join the doctor and his wife. "I understand that your husband told you all about his first journey up here into the mountains. I thought you might succeed in leading us to the gold where he has so miserably failed."

"But, sir—that's totally absurd. I have no idea—why, I can hardly remember what Ralph told me."

"Perhaps your memory will improve," Chase suggested.

Barclay, noting the sly look on the man's face, asked, "Just what is that supposed to mean?"

"I think I might be able to persuade Mrs. Barclay to remember what she claims to have forgotten." Chase's hand dropped to the butt of his gun.

Eva took a step closer to her husband.

Barclay said, "If you touch her, Chase, I'll kill you!"

"With what? Your bare hands?"

Barclay knew he had left his knife at the spot where he had been attacked by the puma. He took Eva's arm, turned away from Chase, and led his wife over to where Pardue was adding wood to the fire.

"Ben, I'd like you to meet my wife. Eva, this is Sergeant Benjamin Pardue. He saved my life back at Fort McDowell." Barclay proceeded to tell Eva about having been jumped by the two soldiers and about Pardue's timely intervention on his behalf.

"I'm pleased to make your acquaintance, Sergeant Pardue," Eva said. "That was a very brave thing you did for my husband. I am as grateful to you for it as he is."

"Anybody with a grain of decency in him would have done the same thing, ma'am."

"So this is the little woman," Betsy said, sauntering up to the trio. "My name's Betsy. I met up with your husband in Phoenix before we all got together and headed here."

Eva gave Barclay an inquisitive glance.

"Ain't she a fine figure of a woman, Chase?" Willy said, pointing at Eva. "I tried getting next to her on the way here, but she wasn't having any of me or what I had to offer her."

This time it was Barclay's turn to give Eva an inquisitive glance.

"I had a strong hankering after her, too," Willy pined, his voice wistful, his eyes roaming up and down Eva's body. "It's been awhile since I had me a woman, Chase. Don't you think the two of us together could get her to give us a little more than the time of day?"

Betsy leered at Willy.

Chase ordered his brother to strip his horse and wipe it down. He said they would be heading out to resume their search as soon as they had breakfast.

As Willy limped away on his crutch, Barclay said, "Chase, you keep that randy brother of yours far away from my wife."

"Maybe I will and maybe I won't," Chase taunted. " Pardue, stoke up that fire. Betsy, I'm hungry. What have we got for breakfast?"

"Boiled beans and baked potatoes," Betsy replied, her thoughtful eyes on Willy, who was removing the saddle from his horse.

"So don't just stand there. Dish it out."

Betsy slowly walked away, never once taking her eyes off Willy until she reached the fire. Then she slowly turned and looked back at Chase, who gestured impatiently at her. She began to spoon beans onto a plate.

Later, when they had finished breakfast, Chase announced that it was time for Mrs. Barclay, as he referred to Eva, to "speak her piece."

Eva glanced anxiously at her husband. "What is it you want me to say?" she asked Chase.

"I want you to tell me all the things your husband told you about his first trip into the mountains with that Indian guide of his. All the details."

When Eva hesitated, biting her lower lip, he said, "It's daylight already. We're wasting time, Mrs. Barclay. Let's hear what you have to say."

"I don't know if I can remember it all. I really didn't pay too much attention to my husband at the time."

"Do the best you can," Chase said. Then, more sharply, he added, "But let me suggest to you that your best had better be good."

Eva looked down at her hands and then up at Chase. "Ralph told me that he and Chunz rode southeast until they reached the Salt River. Ralph said they forded the river near a place he called—what was the name of that place, Ralph?"

"Mormon Flat ford."

"Yes, they forded the Salt River near the Mormon Flat ford. When they reached the mountains, Ralph said they rode past the entrances to a number of canyons that led into the mountains. Then they stopped."

"Go on, Mrs. Barclay," Chase prompted.

"It's difficult for me to remember it all," she said, her brow furrowing. "Let me see now. Oh, yes. Ralph said they stopped at the entrance to one of the canyons and Chunz blindfolded my husband. But before he did so, Ralph said he made it a point to remember the lay of the land around the entrance to the canyon.

"He told me he saw some scrub pine and some ocotillo bushes. There was a creek nearby that formed a waterfall."

"What else?" Chase asked when Eva paused.

She clasped her chin in one hand, closed her eyes, and said, "I remember only one other thing at that point."

"What one other thing?" Chase asked, impatience tightening his voice.

"Ralph said he saw four peaks rising in the west. Then he said Chunz blindfolded him and they rode on."

As Eva went on relating to Chase what she knew of her husband's journey into the Superstitions, Barclay found himself thinking back over what she had just said. Something about her words bothered him. However, exactly what it was that bothered him he didn't know. But he had the nagging feeling that she had said something important.

"Ralph concentrated on trying to remember the various twists and turns the trail took and on what the ground underfoot was like," Eva continued. "At first it was hard, he said. Then it became sandy. He told me he knew they were climbing higher into the mountains as they traveled because the air grew cooler and he could hear the labored breathing of his horse."

Eva went on talking for several more minutes as she described Barclay's account of his and Chunz's journey into the mountains.

"When Chunz later removed my husband's blindfold," she continued, "Ralph said that they headed into a tributary canyon. At first he thought it was what I believe he called a 'box canyon.' But then some time later, he was able to see that it ended in an incline that led down into a valley that he had not been able to see when they first entered the gorge."

"Then what?" Chase asked.

"Ralph saw the gold down in the valley. It was embedded in a ledge of rose quartz, he told me. He gathered some and came home. That's really all I can tell you."

"Are you sure about that, Mrs. Barclay?" Chase asked.

She nodded.

"How long did the whole trip to the valley take?" Chase asked.

"Ralph didn't say, or if he did, I've forgotten."

Barclay answered the question. "I estimate that it took us less than two hours to reach the valley where the gold was from the time we entered the canyon where I saw the four peaks off to the east."

"Ralph, those peaks—you told me they were in the west," Eva interjected.

Barclay suddenly realized what it was that had been bothering him about what Eva had been saying earlier. She had said that he had told her he had seen four peaks in the west. But the peaks had been in the east when he selected the canyon to enter with Chase and the others on their first attempt to locate the gold. He had chosen the wrong canyon!

"I made a mistake," he told Chase. "That canyon we rode into when we first got to the mountains—it was the wrong one because the four peaks were in the east at its entrance point. They should have been in the west."

Chase swore volubly, causing Eva to blush. "You've been wasting my time!" he snarled, glaring at Barclay. "Dammit, Doctor, do you think *now* you can pick out the right canyon to ride into—now that your wife has given me the correct version?"

"I can find the canyon," Barclay said, suppressing the anger that Chase's contemptuous words had stirred in him. "I'm sure I can."

"Then we'll move out and go back to our starting point. Maybe this time Dr. Barclay can get things straight." Chase paused, looking around. "Where are Betsy and Willy?"

When no one answered him, he cupped his hands around his mouth and bellowed, "Willy!"

"Keep the noise down," Pardue told him nervously. "We don't want to tell every Apache from here to kingdom come we're here."

Betsy came running out of the trees at the edge of the campsite. Her dress was torn, her left shoulder bared. She was weeping and cursing at the same time. She turned and shook a fist at the trees. She continued shaking it at Willy as he emerged from the trees, hobbling on his makeshift crutch.

"Willy, you—" Chase started to say.

Betsy interrupted him by shrieking, "That brother of yours just tried to rape me!"

Chase's stare turned stony. He looked at Betsy, then at Willy. "Is that true, boy? Did you have a go at her?"

Before Willy could answer, Betsy cried, "I went into the woods to answer a call of nature. He followed me and grabbed me. I told him I didn't want what he wanted to give me. He said I was going to get it whether I wanted it or not. I tried to fight him off, Chase, but I couldn't."

"Damn you, boy!" Chase snarled. "Damn you for daring to mess with my property!"

"Chase," Willy said, "I didn't. She asked me to go into the woods with her. She said she was tired of listening to all this talk about peaks and bushes and like that. She said she wanted some action."

"That's not true!" Betsy shrilled. "He's lying, Chase!"

"Boy, you've been nothing but a trial and a torment to me since you caught up with me. It's time I was shut of you for good and all. *Draw!*"

"No, Chase, I won't. Chase, what are you fixing to do? You wouldn't shoot your own flesh and blood, would you, Chase?"

"Draw, dammit!"

Willy, his eyes wide with fright, shook his head.

Chase's gun cleared leather. He squeezed off a snap shot that whistled past the left side of his brother's head."

"Chase, *noooooooo!*"

As Willy's last word wailed through the camp, he turned and tried to run to the right at the same instant that Chase fired a second time.

The bullet caught him in the left ear. It spun him around. His crutch fell to the ground as his arms flailed and he struggled desperately to maintain his footing. A moment later he went down and lay motionless on the ground, blood trickling from his wounded ear, the bullet's exit wound on the other side of his head leaking blood and brains.

"I was just trying to throw a scare into him," a startled Chase muttered under his breath. "I wasn't trying to kill him. If he hadn't run like some silly sheep, he wouldn't have had to die like that." He swore and then ordered Barclay to dig a grave.

"Where?" Barclay asked.

"Where doesn't much matter," Chase responded offhandedly. "There where he fell. That's as good a place as any."

As Barclay went to get a shovel from among their supplies, Chase went over and removed the gun from his brother's waistband and placed it in his own. Then he ordered Pardue to pack their gear and provisions on the mules.

"We're moving out," he announced as Barclay began to dig and Pardue headed for the mules.

Eva walked over to where her husband was digging a grave for Willy Ransom. Averting her eyes from the corpse and the ants and flies that had begun already to feed on the drying blood, she said, "That man is absolutely heartless. He acts as if killing his brother was nothing more than a nuisance to him. Why, he isn't even helping to dig his brother's grave."

Barclay nodded. "He's a hard case, no doubt about that." He threw dirt over his shoulder and then rammed the shovel down into the ground again. "Eva, I want to tell you how sorry I am for all this. If I'd ever had any idea that you would become mixed up in this, I swear to you I would never have set foot outside Fort McDowell to search for gold."

"I know that, Ralph." She watched him dig for a moment, and then her eyes slowly shifted to Willy's body. "We are in great danger here, aren't we?" she asked in a voice that was barely audible.

"Yes," Barclay answered bluntly, "we are."

"Tell me how you became involved with Chase and Betsy and the others."

Barclay told her everything, including the parts that reflected on his own lack of judgment.

"I don't blame you, you know," Eva said when he finished speaking. He looked up at her.

"I can understand why you wanted to be with Miss Whitcomb. She's a pretty girl in a brassy sort of way. If I had been more of a wife to you, you wouldn't have had to turn to the likes of her. I suppose Chase is her procurer."

"Yes, he is," Barclay said, continuing to dig. "He's been none too kind or considerate where she's concerned. She sees the gold as a chance to make a new life for herself, and I thought it was the least I could do to help her realize her dreams."

"You were always a generous man, Ralph. Too generous for your own good. You let people take advantage of you."

"I'm afraid you're right."

"I wouldn't have you any other way."

Barclay didn't trust himself to look up at his wife. The softness and warmth of her tone reminded him of the way things had once been between them. He was afraid that, if he looked at her now, he might see something in her eyes that belied her words.

"What are we going to do?" Eva asked.

"Frankly, Eva, I don't know. Ben and I tried to escape the other day, but we didn't get far. Chase caught Ben and then he yelled out that I was to return here to the camp or else he would kill Ben. So I came back. Now the only thing I can think to do is for Ben and me to somehow try to get the drop on Chase."

"I could help. Once you and Sergeant Pardue were ready to overpower him, I could distract Chase with a few well-chosen words and by exercising my feminine wiles. That would give you and Sergeant Pardue your opportunity."

Barclay smiled. "I'm sure you're right. I know when you exercised your feminine wiles on me, I paid very close attention to you, and before I knew what had happened I was married to you."

Barclay climbed up out of the shallow grave he had dug and dropped his shovel. "Eva—" He didn't know what to say, but he wanted to say something that would make her understand that he still loved her and didn't want to lose her. He wanted to touch her, but he was afraid that if he did she would turn away from him, perhaps resenting the feel of his hands on her body.

She surprised and delighted him by stepping close to him and cradling his face in her hands. She gazed into his eyes as if she were searching for something she had lost.

"Eva," he said again and found he could say no more.

"I'm glad Willy brought me here, Ralph."

"Glad?" He couldn't believe what he had heard. How could she be glad about being here in the teeth of danger?

"If Willy hadn't come for me, I would have boarded the east-bound stage and been gone by now, Ralph. I had planned to file for divorce once I reached Boston. I think now that would have been a terrible mistake on my part."

"I love you, Eva." Barclay was amazed at how easily the words came to his lips.

"I love you too, Ralph. I don't know where or when I went astray and misplaced that love, but now that I've found it again, I've discovered that my love for you is even stronger than it was before."

They embraced, holding each other tightly, neither of them saying anything.

"Finish with Willy, Barclay!" Chase yelled. He was standing with an arm around Betsy as her head lolled lazily against his shoulder.

Barclay and Eva parted, and Barclay placed Willy in the grave and began to cover the body with dirt.

Later, as they rode through the canyon, heading for its entrance, no one spoke. Eva was riding Willy's horse beside her husband. Pardue, on Barclay's other side, trailed their two-mule string. Chase, with Betsy at his side, brought up the rear.

Although the sun was rising, it did not illuminate the bottom of the canyon. Purple and black shadows lurked there.

By the time they reached the mouth of the canyon, the sun was high and they rode out of the shadows into a bright, hot world that wrung sweat from their bodies.

"Which one?" Chase snapped, directing his question to Barclay.

Barclay knew what he meant. Without answering, he rode on, following a course parallel to the mountains with the flatland on his right. Chase handed Willy's revolver to Betsy and told her to keep Eva and Pardue under guard. Then he rode out after Barclay.

The two men rode for more than a mile before Barclay finally found what he had been looking for—the mouth of a canyon near which was a creek with a waterfall and from which he could see the four peaks against the sky in the west.

"This one," he said.

Chase gestured and they rode back to join the others. Then the entire group headed for the canyon that Barclay had pointed out to Chase.

Betsy began to hum merrily as they entered the canyon. Two hours later she was too weary to hum as Barclay held up a hand to call a halt.

The canyon they were in had angled off from its original direction so that now it ran in a north–south direction. The western wall looming above them was formed by the cliffs of a mountain range.

"This is it?" Chase asked eagerly, heeling his horse and riding up next to Barclay.

"No"

"What the hell—"

"There," Barclay interrupted, pointing to a tributary canyon some distance ahead of them.

Chase rode up to it, turned his horse, and rode back to the others. "That canyon dead-ends a hundred yards in. I didn't see any sign of gold in there. What—"

"We ride in," Barclay said firmly. "It's not a box canyon. Once we get in far enough, we'll be able to see a valley that you can't see from the canyon's entrance."

As Barclay moved his horse out, Chase said, "Hold it, Doctor!"

Barclay drew rein and looked back over his shoulder at Chase, who said, "I'm going in alone." Turning to Betsy, he said, "You keep your eyes and that gun on this bunch. Don't let them try anything on you. If you let them jump you and they don't kill you, I will when I get back."

"Chase, why don't you just shut that loud mouth of yours?" she responded. "You go on about your business and I'll tend to mine."

Chase galloped away without another word.

Chapter Twelve

"Keep your distance!" Betsy ordered, brandishing the gun that Chase had given her and forcing the others to back away from her.

She seated herself on a flat rock and, holding the gun in both hands, said, "Don't any of you try anything fancy. If you do, I'll shoot. I swear I will. It don't make no difference to me if I have to kill the whole lot of you. That will just leave that much more gold for Chase and me."

"She'll do it for sure," Pardue said in a low tone to Barclay, who stood with his arm around Eva's waist. "She's got the gleam in her eyes that means she's keen on killing."

"I'll talk to her," Barclay said. "Try to reason with her." Turning to Eva, he said, "Stay here. I'll be right back."

As he took a step toward Betsy, she rose. "Are you fixing to be the first one to die, Doc?"

"Betsy, listen to me," Barclay said, halting. "You're betting your money on the wrong horse. You shouldn't be siding with Chase against us."

Betsy laughed harshly. "You've got that all wrong, Doc. I'm not on Chase's side, I'm on *my* side."

"Betsy, once Chase is sure of the gold's location, he's going to come back here, and I think"—Barclay lowered his voice in the hope that Eva would not hear his next words—"he's going to kill us all."

"You really think Chase would kill me?"

"I do, yes."

"You're wrong about that. I can take care of myself."

"Betsy, my guess is that Chase wants that gold all to himself. What reason would he have to divide it with anyone?

"None." Barclay answered his own question emphatically, "But if the four of us were to band together against him—"

"It's easy to see that you're holding a losing hand, Doc. You're making a wild play. Well, it won't work. Not with me, it won't."

"Give me the gun."

"Give you the gun?" Betsy cried, her tone incredulous. "Give you the gun?" she repeated mockingly. Then, teasingly, "What would you do with it, Doc, if I were dumb enough to give it to you? Would you kill Chase with it?"

"No, I wouldn't kill Chase. I would use it to get the drop on him."

"Then what?"

"Then I'd take him back to Phoenix and turn him over to the proper authorities."

"The proper authorities," Betsy repeated, her voice oozing sarcasm. "*This* is the proper authority, Doc, don't you know that?" She brandished the gun.

"Miss Whitcomb," Eva said as she suddenly appeared at Barclay's side. "My husband is right in what he has told you. None of us are going to survive once Chase knows for certain where the gold is. He will murder us all, you very much included. But if you give us the gun, we will all have a good chance of staying alive."

Betsy's lips curled in a sneer. "That's always the way of it, isn't it? People like you trying to make people like me do what you want. Well, Mrs. High and Mighty, I'm not having any, so you and your husband can go back and sit down and *shut up!*"

"Betsy, it's not like that at all," Barclay protested. "Didn't I agree to take you on this trip? Wasn't I willing to share the gold with you? You can't turn around now and claim that I in any way used or exploited you. It simply is not true and flies in the face of reality."

"You did me a good turn, Doc," Betsy said in a somewhat softer tone. "I admit it and I thank you for it. There aren't many men in the world who would have done for me what you did."

"Then—"

Betsy silenced Barclay with a stony stare and continued, "But things have changed since then. Chase has joined the party. Maybe what you say is true. Maybe he does intend to kill you folks. I wouldn't put it past him. But that only makes me see that I have to look out for my own self no matter which way the wind takes to blowing. So you all move back. Don't try to jump me as I'd no doubt get to kill one or two of you before you got me."

Barclay, realizing that he would get nowhere with Betsy, retreated with Eva.

"You did your best," Eva said, as they sat down together next to the canyon wall.

"It wasn't good enough, sad to say," a dejected Barclay responded. "Eva, I didn't want you to hear what they have planned for us."

"I think I knew almost from the moment I arrived with Willy. When I realized that I had been duped into coming here and then learned why I had been duped, I knew then what Chase had in store for us. I knew the kind of man he was and that he had no intention of sharing the gold with anyone."

"I should never have come back here," Barclay said mournfully. "If I had been content with the gold I found initially, all would now be well."

"I'm not so sure about that, Ralph."

"What do you mean?"

"Do you really think all would have been well if you had merely remained at Fort McDowell?"

"You mean between us?"

"Yes. What I'm getting at is this. When Willy told me you were badly hurt and near death, something happened to me. It continued happening to me during the long journey here to the mountains. I felt as if I, too, were badly hurt and near death. I felt empty and bereft."

"I could kill Chase for putting you through this."

"I've learned from the experience, Ralph."

"Learned?"

"I've learned to seek out and hold on to the precious things in life and to separate them from the things that are unimportant.

"Our love is a very precious thing and I roundly chastised myself for having let it be damaged by my emphasis on things that are of relatively little value."

Barclay's heart leaped inside him. His spirits soared. He swallowed hard but didn't trust himself to speak.

"Of what possible importance is the wind and the dust it brings into one's domicile?" Eva continued, her face radiant. "Of what conceivable significance is the fact that we must spend another year in a desolate frontier outpost such as Fort McDowell? We have years ahead of us, Ralph. We have most of our lives left to live"

"I, too, have learned since this misadventure began," Barclay said, taking his wife's hand. "I've learned the profound truth of the verse from Proverbs: 'Pride goeth before destruction, and an haughty spirit before a fall.' "

Barclay regretted the words as soon as they left his mouth. "I didn't mean— We'll come out of this all right. I feel sure we will."

She silenced him with a smile and a soft finger on his lips. "I know what you meant, Ralph. You let your pride lead you to turn away from me and pursue your dream of riches."

"Pursue my folly, is more like it," a rueful Barclay declared.

"You mustn't condemn yourself. I think, were I in your place, I would have done the very same thing. If I were you and found myself confronted by a headstrong and immature woman incapable of facing up to minor hardships, I definitely would have come here to the mountains to search for another kind of gold, since my wife seemed incapable of enjoying the golden treasure of love I had already given her."

"Eva." It was all Barclay could manage to say. He threw his arms around his wife and held her close.

Then, withdrawing and holding her at arm's length, he said solemnly, "I can't promise you we will find a satisfactory way out of this situation, Eva, but I can promise you that I will try my level best to see that we do survive."

They embraced again, and this time their lips met.

"Sorry to butt in, Captain," Pardue said, "but here comes Chase, and he sure don't look like a happy man."

Barclay and Eva drew apart and Barclay stared into the distance at Chase and the small cloud of dust he was rising as he galloped toward them. "Ben," he said quietly, "we've got to make a move. We've got to try to get our guns away from him."

"I reckon you're right, Captain. Have you got some sort of plan in mind?"

"No, I'm afraid I don't. But let's be on the alert. Maybe we'll get an opportunity to turn the tables on him."

"I hope we do, Captain."

"Was it there?" Betsy called out as she leaped to her feet. "Did you find the gold?" she cried as she ran to meet Chase.

He rode past her, the dust he was raising causing her to cough violently.

He drew rein in front of Barclay and snapped, "There was no valley in that canyon, Doctor. There was no gold there either."

Before Barclay could say anything, Betsy came running up to them, gun in hand. "Show me some gold, Chase. Oh, let me see that gold shine and glitter."

Chase dismounted, shoved Betsy to one side, and stood directly in front of Barclay, his right hand on the butt of his gun. "Doctor, would you like to know what I think? I think you're stalling. I think you've been stalling all along. I think you've been running our tails all over this goddamn wilderness and all the while you never took us anywhere even *near* that gold!"

"That's not true," Barclay said as calmly as he could, although Chase's words had stirred fear in his heart. "I've made every effort to find the gold. Are you sure you looked carefully in that canyon?"

Chase snorted derisively. "Did I look carefully? Doctor, I looked high and I looked low and I looked in between. No valley, no vein, no gold nowhere."

"You must be mistaken."

"I'm not!" an enraged Chase screamed shrilly, his face flushing, the cords in his neck growing taut.

The fear Barclay had been feeling intensified. Chase seemed ready to explode.

"I'll go and search," he volunteered and then, seeing the hard look Chase gave him, amended his statement by saying, *"We'll* go and look. I'm sure I can prove to you that you're wrong."

"There isn't any gold?" Betsy said in a small voice, her words a lament.

"That's right," Chase said without looking at her. "There's no gold and soon there will be no Dr. Barclay."

"What are you fixing to do, Chase?" Betsy asked, suddenly apprehensive. "Chase, now don't you go and do something you're sure to be sorry for."

"Oh, I won't do that, my dear Betsy. But I will do something that will make me very happy. I will shoot holes in the hide of this conniving, deceitful son of a bitch."

"Don't, Chase!" Betsy pleaded, seizing Chase's arm, the gun in her other hand hanging at her side.

He shook her off. "I'm not going to waste any more of my valuable time with this bastard," he muttered, his eyes drilling into Barclay.

"Don't you dare hurt my husband!" Eva cried, stepping in front of Barclay to protect him.

Chase reached out, seized her by the shoulder, and flung her to one side.

146

"Damn you, Chase!" Barclay exclaimed angrily as Eva fell to the ground, her hair coming undone. He lunged at Chase.

Chase struck him with a fist, opening Barclay's head wound.

The doctor was whirled around by the blow. His hand went to his head, which was alive with pain that practically blinded him. He heard Eva call his name. He saw a hand—was it Pardue's?—reach out to steady him. He fell anyway.

Pardue bent down to help him up. At the same time Eva got to her feet and came over to him. She gave him a handkerchief to help stanch the blood that was flowing from the reopened wound.

Then Barclay was on his feet again, holding his wife's handkerchief over his wound, and Eva was helping to support him while Pardue flanked him on the opposite side.

"Chase, go with Doc," Betsy urged, tugging at the man's arm. "Maybe he knows how to find the gold. Maybe you missed it. Chase, don't you see? If you kill him, neither one of us will ever get our hands on any of that gold!"

"No!" Chase's word thundered in the air.

"Yes!" Betsy's word was a desperate shriek.

She backed away from Chase. The gun in her hand rose slowly and seemingly of its own volition. "Chase, you listen to me now and you listen good. If you try to shoot Doc, I'm going to drill you, so help me."

Chase nodded. Watching her intently, he looked like a snake trying to mesmerize a bird. "You fool!" he snapped. "You dare to turn on me. Well, I won't have a slut like you turn a gun on her betters."

Eva screamed as Chase's gun cleared leather. She screamed a second time as Betsy fired and Chase, an expression of complete surprise on his face, bent forward, his body doubling over and the gun falling from his hand. "No," he said with a sigh. "No," he moaned again and then crumpled to the ground.

Barclay sprang. He got a grip on the wrist of Betsy's gun hand and shoved her arm up so that her gun was aiming harmlessly at the sky. He twisted her wrist as hard as he could.

She screamed in pain and dropped her gun.

Barclay bent and scooped it up.

She made a sudden grab for it and succeeded in wresting it from Barclay, who was taken by surprise by her unexpected move.

"I'll get her, Captain!" Pardue shouted and moved in on Betsy.

But before Pardue could lay a hand on Betsy, Barclay was again struggling to repossess her weapon.

It fired.

Betsy staggered backward for several paces and then fell, blood bursting from a wound on the right side of her chest.

Barclay stood there, stunned, as he stared down at Betsy. Then, recovering himself, he knelt and took her wrist in his hand, feeling for a pulse.

"Betsy, I'm sorry. I didn't mean to—"

"I know. My fault."

Barclay, a feeling of helplessness flooding him, ripped the sleeve of his shirt and used the material to stem the blood flowing from Betsy's chest.

Her right hand rose from the ground and fell feebly back. "Chase?"

Barclay turned. Pardue was bending over the supine figure of Chase Ransom. The sergeant looked up at Barclay and shook his head.

"He's gone, Betsy," Barclay murmured.

"Good. He—" Betsy sounded as if she were gargling. Blood welled from her mouth, reddening her lips. "He would have tried to take all the gold. Serves him right."

Barclay watched as a bloody froth bubbled past Betsy's lips and flowed down her chin and cheeks.

"—smart, Doc."

"What did you say?" Barclay asked, bending closer.

"You tricked us all. Led us down the garden path. But not to the gold."

"Betsy, I didn't. I tried to find the gold. I really did."

"Joke's on us. On Chase and Willy and me."

Betsy whispered something else, but although Barclay strained to catch her words, he could not make them out.

"Wouldn't I have been magnificent, Doc? With all the gold turned into cold cash and me the richest woman in the West?"

"Yes, Betsy," Barclay replied. "You would have been magnificent, indeed."

"And free at last to be whatever I wanted to be."

"Yes."

"Free, Doc, free . . ."

No more blood came from Betsy's chest wound. None slipped past her lips. Barclay knew her heart had stopped pumping. Looking up at Pardue and then at Eva, he said, "She's dead."

He closed Betsy's sightless eyes and stood up. "I killed her."

"Ralph," Eva said, putting an arm around his waist, "it was an accident."

"I never should have let her come on this trip. It's my fault that she's dead." Barclay's voice was sepulchral, his tone haunted.

"Mrs. Barclay's right, Captain," Pardue said. "You didn't kill her. The gun went off accidentally."

"The gold," Barclay said, his eyes fixed on nothing. *"Goddamn the gold!"* he roared, his voice returning to him in ghostly echoes as it ricocheted off the canyon walls.

"Goddamn
the
gold, gold, gold, gold!"

His shoulders slumped as he buried his face in his hands.

Eva held him close, saying nothing as sobs shook his body.

When he quieted, she said, "Are you all right now?"

Instead of answering, Barclay looked up and said, "We're going home now."

Eva nodded.

"Ben, bring Chase's and Betsy's horses here. We'll put the bodies on them."

"Did I hear you right before, Captain? Did you say you were heading back to the fort?"

"That's right."

"But what about the gold."

"What about it?"

"You're not giving up the hunt for it, are you now, Captain?"

"I am. I want nothing more to do with the gold. Let the thunder gods have it. They're welcome to it, as far as I'm concerned."

Pardue, a grim expression on his face, turned on his heels and went to get the horses. On the way back, he picked up the two guns Chase and Betsy had dropped. He gave one to Barclay, who thrust it into his waistband, and kept the other one for himself.

When they had loaded the two lifeless bodies on the horses, Barclay turned to Eva. "Are you ready, my dear?"

"Yes."

As Eva walked toward her horse, Barclay noticed that she was limping. "What's the matter with your leg?"

"I hurt my ankle when Chase knocked me down. I expect it's sprained, but I can manage."

"Here, let me have a look at it."

Eva sat down on a rock, and Barclay knelt in front of her and unlaced her shoe. He deftly examined her left ankle, causing her to wince in pain despite the care he took.

"It's not broken, just sprained, as you said. But you really should stay off it a while."

"I can ride, Ralph. And I am anxious to get back to the fort."

"But the captain's right, Mrs. Barclay," Pardue interjected. "You don't favor that ankle of yours, it'll wind up giving you a peck of trouble you can avoid if you just give it a nice rest. It's already swollen up to the size of a small balloon."

Eva looked at her ankle and then at Barclay. "It does hurt rather severely at the moment," she admitted. "But I don't want to be a bother. I—"

"We'll spend the night here," Barclay announced. "We can leave in the morning. Meanwhile I'll prepare some compresses to put on your ankle which should reduce the swelling. The pain will lessen in time."

"Captain," Pardue said, "while you're busy seeing to your missus, I think I'll meander into that canyon yonder and see what I can see. Chase may have been all wet about there not being gold in it."

But when Pardue returned some time later, his visage was glum. As Barclay and Eva looked at him expectantly, he shook his head and said, "There's not a grain of gold in that canyon, Captain."

"You're sure?" Barclay questioned him.

"I went over the place with a fine-tooth comb and there's not a trace of gold to be found there."

"It's not that I doubt you, Ben, but I think I'll have a look myself, if you'll stay here with Mrs. Barclay."

"Go ahead, Captain."

Barclay returned with the same bleak appraisal as had Chase and Pardue. There was no gold in the canyon.

"I must have chosen the wrong canyon again," he said. "Well, such is the luck of the prospector, I suppose."

Pardue said nothing for a moment, then suggested, "It seems a shame to give up the search now, Captain, it really does. I mean we're here and the gold's here somewhere."

"I'm sorry to disappoint you, Ben, but I'll tell you what I'll do. As soon as we get back to Fort McDowell, I'll draw a map that you can use as a starting point if you want to go gold hunting sometime in the future. Maybe you'll have more luck at it than I have had."

"I do appreciate your willingness to do that, Captain. It shows you to be a generous man, which is something I've known about you since we first met. But I'm not sure a map would do me much good. You're the one who went and got the gold the first time out. A map wouldn't work near as well as your own sharp eyes."

"My eyes, sharp or not, haven't done us much good so far. The problem is that things tend to look the same up here."

Pardue sat down with his back braced against the canyon wall. He folded his arms across his upraised knees. Closing his eyes and leaning his head against the stone wall behind him, he said, "It's the dream of a wild boyo I had in my mind all this time. I was going to find that gold and stuff my pockets and my hat full of it, and then in the long years ahead, I was going to indulge my every whim and fancy, I was."

He opened his eyes. "Do you know, Captain, I was going to go to California after I got the gold and left the army? I was going to see the ocean. Me, Benjamin Pardue, was going to buy a nice little house to settle down in and then find a nice wife to live with, and everything was going to be honey and wine from that day on.

"Now I guess I'll not be hearing the lapping of the California ocean waves after all. Which is fine and dandy. I'll get along. I always have.

"You know, Captain, you are a lucky man. When you leave the service and go back to—where was it you said you and Mrs. Barclay hailed from?"

"Boston."

"When you get back to Boston and get all set up as a doctor there, why, you'll be a rich man before you know it. You're fortunate indeed to have a skill such as yours. Being a doctor and healing the sick, it's a fine profession.

"So the gold is best forgotten. You tried your best to find it, Captain. What more could anybody expect you to do?"

"Ben, I'm truly sorry to have let you down so badly," Barclay said.

"Think no more about it, Captain."

"In a way," Barclay mused, "it does seem a shame to give up without trying to find the gold one last time."

"You could do it, Captain," Pardue said in an encouraging voice. "I know you could."

"Ralph," Eva said uneasily, "I really think you should give up the search and come home."

Barclay patted her arm. "I owe Ben a great deal, Eva. He saved my life, as I told you earlier." Turning to Pardue, he said, "Ben, I'll make a deal with you. If you'll look after Mrs. Barclay, I'll go out again."

"You mean you're going to give it another try, Captain?"

"Yes, one last try. If I'm not successful this time—that will be it. Agreed, Ben?"

"Agreed. Bless you, Captain. I think this time you'll do it."

Chapter Thirteen

Hours later, when Barclay galloped into camp, his horse was sweaty and blown and his eyes were wild with fright.

"What's wrong, Captain?" Pardue asked as he hurried over to where Barclay was dismounting. "You look like the devil himself's on your back trail."

"Apaches!" Barclay gasped as he ran to where Eva was sitting in the shade.

Pardue ran after him. "Apaches, you say? Where are the bloody heathens?"

"Somewhere behind me," Barclay muttered through clenched teeth. "Eva, we must leave here at once. I ran into some Apaches back along the trail." Barclay looked up at Pardue. "You remember Eskiminzin and the three men he had with him? You remember Torres, the Angel of Death?"

Pardue nodded.

"It was Eskiminzin and his companions who chased and nearly caught me. But I was fortunate. I took cover and they rode past me. I waited, and when they didn't come back, I rode back here as fast as I could."

"Apaches," Pardue breathed. He swore.

"They're expert trackers," Barclay declared grimly. At the same time Eva got to her feet and he helped her walk toward her horse. "They'll find us sooner or later," he continued. "And when they do, they'll kill us."

"They won't find or kill me," Pardue said sharply. "You and the missus maybe, Captain, but not me."

"What do you mean?" Barclay asked as he halted with Eva next to her horse.

"What do I mean?" Pardue strode over to them.

"This is what I mean. I came up here into these mountains for gold because I wanted to be a rich man, Captain. I had that wanting in mind the night those two men jumped you back at Fort McDowell.

"I told you then I had followed them out of the sutler's store because I thought they might be meaning you harm. Well, Captain, it just so happens that what I really had in mind was to beat them to you, only they got to you first."

"But I thought—"

"You thought I was on the prowl to save you like I claimed. Not so. I lied to you, Captain. I meant to have that eleven thousand dollars you boasted you got from the quartermaster."

A dazed Barclay asked, "Then why didn't you rob me after you had routed the other two men who had attacked me?"

"Because, Captain, I suddenly had a much better idea. Granted that it was a gamble—"

"You thought I'd be so grateful to you for saving my life that I'd share my bonanza with you," Barclay said as understanding came to him.

"And that's exactly what you volunteered to do, didn't you?"

"I did," Barclay murmured sadly, "and it would appear now that I was a fool for doing so."

"But then you almost pulled a fast one that put my hopes for the future in jeopardy, Captain."

Barclay looked at Pardue expectantly.

"Your escape plan, Captain," the sergeant explained.

"What about it?"

"When you came up with that idea, I could see the goose that was going to lay me a golden egg was getting ready to fly away.

"I had to stop you, and do it fast. But how?

"I came up with the idea of telling Chase what you were fixing to do so he would be on the alert to foil your plan. So what did I do? I volunteered to get him to agree to me picketing the horses away from our campsite. I told you that way we would be able to make our getaway without making noise. Do you remember that, Captain?"

"I remember that you went over to talk to Chase."

"That's when I told him what you were planning. I told him I was ready to throw in with him and the others against you. He went for it."

"You were going to help me climb aboard your horse," Barclay said. "Why did you do that if you wanted Chase to capture me?"

"I did it to make the escape look legitimate. If you'd gotten on my horse, I would have seen to it that Chase eventually caught us one way or the other."

"If Chase hadn't captured me, I suppose you would have tracked me to Weaver's Needle, where you said we'd meet after we split up."

"That's about the size of it, Captain. But then when Chase and I got together after you'd run off, I had a better idea. It was my idea to have him yell out an order for you to come back to the camp or else Chase would kill me. By God, didn't it work, though? Back you came with your tail tucked between your legs to save the friend we bamboozled you into thinking was in danger."

"You would have lost your gamble in the end," Barclay said sadly. "Chase would have killed you. Betsy, too. Willy as well, had he lived."

"You've got that all wrong, Captain. Chase wasn't going to

kill Betsy and Willy. He was just going to give them the slip, he told me, just like he'd done to his brother in Kansas City, only this time he planned to get rid of both of them for good and all.

"As for Chase killing me—you're wrong about that, too. He never would have gotten the chance. I'd have done for him first just like I'd planned to do all along, only it wasn't necessary, seeing as how things turned out."

"This is a fine way you chose to repay me for my offer to share the gold with you, Ben, a fine way indeed."

"Oh, now, don't you go and get pious with me, Captain. What we're about here is business, pure and simple. Where business is concerned, there's no friendship, only the true-blooded American virtue of making as much money as you can. Which is just what I set out to do.

"But I also had a wild card tucked away just in case things didn't work out. You don't know where the gold is, and now you've got a bunch of Apache braves on the warpath after you, so it looks like it's time for me to play my wild card."

"I don't know what you mean."

"Then I'll tell you in plain terms. When we started out to search for the gold, I made up my mind that, should things turn sour, I'd settle for a green bird in the hand rather than two gold ones in the bush. I'll settle, Captain, for the eleven thousand dollars you were in such proud possession of that night in the sutler's store."

As Barclay went for his gun, Pardue's gun cleared leather, and the sergeant held out his left hand.

Barclay reluctantly drew his revolver and handed it to Pardue.

"Now then, Captain, hand over that eleven thousand dollars you're packing."

"No," Barclay said, taking two unsteady steps backward.

"Ah, now, Captain, is it getting shot you're after? That does seem a bit foolish. I venture to say that your woman feels the same way about it, don't you, Mrs. Barclay? You don't want to see your husband shot full of holes over his eleven-thousand-dollar bonanza, do you now?"

"Ralph, give him the money," Eva said in a strained voice.

"No," Barclay said, shaking his head.

Pardue fired over the doctor's head, causing Barclay to flinch and Eva to cry out in alarm.

"Please, Ralph," she pleaded. "Give him the money. Then he'll let us go. You will, won't you, Sergeant?"

"Upon my word of honor, I will do that very thing, Mrs. Barclay," Pardue promised unctuously. "Now why don't you do your level best to stop your husband from acting like a foolish man. Tell him to turn his poke over to me."

"Ralph, do as he says."

When Barclay saw the fear in Eva's eyes, he sighed and said, "You win, Ben." He thrust a hand into his pocket. When he withdrew it, a five-dollar bill fell on the ground. So did a small piece of rose quartz that was streaked with gold.

Pardue stared at it, transfixed. Then he moved closer to Barclay, bent down, and picked up the quartz. He turned it over and over in his hand, his lips parting in a wolfish grin. He held the quartz over his head, letting the sun's rays strike it and make the gold flecks glitter and gleam.

Then, lowering his arm and glaring at Barclay, he said, "You found the gold and you never said so, you sneaky son of a bitch."

"You never gave me a chance," Barclay retorted angrily.

"When did you find it? Yesterday? The day before?"

"No. Just now. Just before I stumbled into the path of the Apaches."

"Ralph," Eva said, "we've got to get out of here before those Indians track us down."

"She's right, Ben. We've got to get out of here, and I mean right now. We've already wasted enough time."

"We haven't wasted one minute, not one second of time," Pardue crowed, holding the quartz up to the sunlight again. "But you're right. We've got to get out of here. We've got to go to where the gold is."

"No!" Eva cried as Barclay said, "Ben, that's crazy!"

"It isn't crazy," Pardue argued. "It makes sense. I'll be

damned if I'm going to let a few renegade savages stand between me and all the gold. We'll leave the mules and the packs and those two dead bodies. We'll travel real light."

"Ben, you saw what those Apaches did to Angel Torres," Barclay persisted.

"But they caught Torres. They won't catch us."

"Ralph," Eva whispered in a stricken voice, "I'm frightened."

So was Barclay, but he didn't say so.

"Hand over that money!" Pardue ordered. When the doctor had given him what remained of the eleven thousand dollars, he stuffed it into his pocket and said, "Let's ride!"

Barclay reluctantly helped Eva board her horse. Then he stepped into his saddle.

"Lead on, Captain!" Pardue exclaimed gleefully from behind him as he reholstered his gun. "Lead on to El Dorado!"

The sun was low in the sky when they rode through the canyon Barclay had discovered on his own. Later they rode into a tributary canyon and then up a steep grade that seemed to lead directly to a massive rock wall below overhanging cliffs. But as they came closer to the seemingly impenetrable barrier, they reached a hidden incline that led down to a small valley.

"This is it?" Pardue asked eagerly when Barclay drew rein.

"Down there," Barclay said and pointed.

Pardue peered in the direction the doctor had indicated. "I don't see anything," he said in a surly voice.

"There. To the left. Don't you see the way the sun strikes that low ledge?"

"By God in His heaven, that's gold down there!" Pardue cried in awe.

Barclay moved his horse closer to Eva's. "We've got to be ready to make a run for it," he whispered to her. "Now that he knows where the gold is, he'll have no further use for me."

"You think he's going to kill us?" Eva asked in a low voice, her eyes on Pardue's back as the sergeant rode partway down the incline to the vein of rose quartz.

"I'll say when," Barclay told her without answering her question.

"You, did it, Captain!" Pardue shouted, turning his horse so he was facing Barclay and Eva again. "Now, let's you and me go on down there and *dig*!"

Without a word, Barclay moved his horse out, heading toward Pardue, who sat waiting for him. "Stay behind me," he whispered to Eva from between barely parted lips.

She obediently dropped back as they prepared to start down the slope into the valley below.

Barclay turned his horse and crossed behind Pardue, intending to make a try at seizing the sergeant's revolver. He rode up on Pardue's right, bracing himself for the move he knew he had to make. Glancing back over his shoulder, he made certain that Eva was far enough behind so that she would be out of the line of fire should anything go wrong.

Barclay's hand left his reins. It reached out toward Pardue . . .

. . . who chose that moment to slam his boot heels into the flanks of his mount and go galloping down the slope into the valley.

Barclay, at first surprised by Pardue's move, quickly realized this was the time to make a run for it. *"Now!"* he shouted to Eva.

She turned her horse expertly and began riding back the way they had come, and Barclay followed closely.

Loose granite made the going difficult. Their horses slid and slipped but managed to stay on their feet.

"Hurry!" Barclay called out to Eva, who was several yards ahead of him. His urging was unnecessary. She widened the distance between them.

They had left the ridge above the valley far behind when they heard a scream.

"What was that?" Eva asked breathlessly.

Barclay didn't know. Was Pardue enraged at their escape attempt? Was it Pardue who had screamed or someone else?

"I'm going back," he called to Eva.

"No, Ralph, don't!"

"Maybe Pardue's in trouble. Maybe he needs help. You go on, Eva. Head for home. I'll catch up with you."

"Ralph!" she called out as he turned his horse and galloped back toward the rock wall looming in the distance.

When he reached the ridge from which he could look down into the valley, he dismounted and hid his horse in a grove of alders. Then he lay down on his stomach on the stony ground. Looking into the valley below, he saw a sight that chilled his blood. Eskiminzin and the other three Apaches were almost on Pardue. One of the Indians reached out and ripped an arrow from Pardue's back, causing the sergeant to scream in pain. Then all four Apaches overpowered Pardue and proceeded to strip him of his clothes.

Minutes later the sergeant, despite his struggles, was staked to the ground, his arms and legs spread wide. Standing off to one side, Eskiminzin went through Pardue's pockets. Suddenly, he let out a wild whoop and held up the piece of quartz for the others to see. Then, a moment later, he whooped again and brandished the nearly eleven thousand dollars he had discovered.

Barclay stiffened when he heard the sound of hoofbeats behind him. He quickly took cover behind a manzanita bush. He felt a mixture of relief and anxiety when Eva rode into sight. He stood up and went to her, holding a finger to his lips. He helped her dismount and indicated that she was to lie down on the ridge as he had been doing. Then he led her horse to the stand of trees where he had earlier left his own mount.

When he returned to her, she was looking down into the valley.

Eskiminzin, thrusting the money into one of his tall moccasins and tossing away the piece of quartz, drew a knife as the other three Indians had already done. All four men stood over Pardue, whose lips were working as his gaze darted from one to another of the men.

Barclay could not hear what Pardue was saying. A moment later, he wished he could not hear the man's agonized screams as one of the Apaches knelt beside him and made a circular incision in his right shoulder and then proceeded to slowly flay that arm.

Barclay shuddered at the sight of the skinned arm, all red flesh, gray-white sinew, and blue-white bone. Had he been witnessing an operation of a similar sort with the patient mercifully put under, he would not have shuddered. But to see this torture—to hear Pardue's harrowing screams . . .

Pardue went on screaming as his left arm was slowly skinned.

Eva sobbed, and Barclay put an arm around her. "There's nothing I can do," he moaned. "I have no gun. If I had a gun . . ."

His next words were muffled by the sound of distant thunder.

The sky darkened overhead. From time to time lightning pierced the clouds.

One of Eskiminzin's men built a fire, and the torture continued. Pardue's screams became weaker, his desperate but futile struggles to escape the knives—all four were flaying various parts of his body now—diminished. He lay there, only his head moving slowly from side to side, his screams turned into moans that were barely audible.

"You shouldn't have come back," Barclay told Eva as she began to retch. "I'm sorry you had to see this."

"I was afraid to go on alone," she murmured when the spasms finally subsided. "I wanted to be with you."

"Those Apaches laid an ambush," Barclay said. "They were waiting for me to return to the gold. They knew why I was here in the mountains. Chunz warned me he had told them why he was taking me to the gold. He alerted me afterward that they would kill me if I were to come back again. So, when they lost my trail earlier, they simply went back to the gold to wait for my greed to lead me back to it."

"Ralph!"

As Eva gripped his arm tightly, Barclay looked down again at the group of figures illuminated by the firelight below.

"He's dead," Eva breathed.

Barclay saw that she was right. Pardue lay motionless now, not a shred of skin left on him. The firelight danced obscenely on the ruin of his body, red on ghastly red.

"We have to go," Eva said urgently, almost hysterically, as she started to ride. "They'll come after us now."

Barclay reached up and pulled her back down beside him.

"I don't think that's what they intend to do. Look."

Both of them watched as one of the Apaches untied their victim and then dragged Pardue's corpse into the midst of some creosote bushes, where it could not be seen by anyone approaching the spot. They watched Eskiminzin gesture, and then the three men with him obediently took up positions again behind boulders and a palo verde tree. Eskiminzin then kicked out the fire, scattered its ashes, and took cover with his companions.

Stillness filled the valley. Stillness and a growing darkness that was illuminated from time to time by chain lightning that occasionally struck a jutting mountain peak.

"They're waiting for me to arrive," Barclay said, his voice hoarse from tension. "That's why they hid Pardue's body—so it wouldn't spook me. They believe I'll be back."

He rose as rain began to fall, and he helped Eva over to their horses.

As they rode through the rain on their way down out of the mountains, thunder cannonaded, deafening them. When its roar faded away, Barclay said, "The thunder gods. They're warning us to stay away from their gold."

"We will," Eva said firmly, glancing at her husband. The rain had made a wet mat of her hair and soaked her clothes. "We don't need their gold," she added. "We have something much better. We have each other. That's treasure enough for me."